Hood Love 4: Loving A Carter

Leondra LeRae'

Prologue

Capo

Jonnae walked around the house for an hour just staring at her engagement ring. She called Michelle and Boog to brag about the proposal . I could hear Michelle screaming into the phone as Jonnae squealed. Seeing the smile on her face, warmed my heart and made me want to love her harder.

"Hold on, , let me call Jass," Nae said. She pulled the phone away from her ear and quickly dialed Jass' number.

"Jasmine?" she said. "Hold on." Nae pulled the phone away from her ear and connected the two calls . Watching the excitement in her eyes made me happy. She told Jass about the engagement and she began squealing again. I heard whining so I left Nae to her girl talk and went to tend to the kids.

Walking into the living room, I noticed Janiylah was on

the couch asleep and the twins were on the floor. Kiyra was awoke and in her crawling stance. She saw me and gave me, a drool filled smile.

"Come here daddy's girl." I said as I bent down to pick her up. I felt her full diaper and headed to her room so I could change her. A few minutes later, I went back to the living room to find Kahri sitting up and staring at the blank television screen. I placed Kiyra on the floor beside him and powered on the television for them to watch cartoons. Before I could change the channel, the news broadcasted a story that caught my attention.

I watched as a news reporter stood in front of a house surrounded by yellow crime scenetape, cops and ambulances.

"Baby, what ar-…"

Jonnae stopped mid- sentence as her eyes landed on the television screen as well.

"Turn it up," she said as she made her way next to me.

"I'm standing here outside of 2451 Miller Ave in Providence where it seems a gruesome murder has taken place. Police are canvasing the scene for any evidence. The victim has not yet been identified and no witnesses have come forward. Police ask that anybody with any information either call Crime Stoppers or the Providence Police Department. I'm Donna Davis reporting live with ABC6 news. Back to you, John."

Jonnae's hand was over her mouth in a state of shock while my eyes were glued on the television.

"That's Erick's house," Jonnae whispered. "Capo, what's gon-."

I put my hand up, to signal her to be quiet. I didn't need

her freaking out right now. I was confused because I had distinctly told Rell and Boog to call the clean- up crew. The fact that the body was still at the house meant somebody fucked up. I quickly changed the channel and put the remote on the coffee table. I turned around to find Jonnae standing with tears streaming down her face.

I grabbed her into my arms to calm her down.

"Shh, stop crying Ma. It's gonna be fine," I told her. I had to remain strong although inside of was fuming. She cried into my chest for over five minutes as we stood in the kitchen. Somebody fucked up and somebody needed to tell me why.

Chapter One

Jonnae

It didn't matter how much Capo tried to calm me down, my gut was telling me that this shit wouldn't end good. This wasn't like Capo, he wasn't messy. I know he wouldn't have left the body there for somebody to find, so I was confused.

"Babe, what happened," I asked him. The look in his eyes spoke volumes. Although he tried to hide it, I could tell that he was nervous.

"Man, I don't know, but I'm going to find the fuck out." He pulled away from me and went into the bedroom. A few minutes later, he returned dressed in all black. The only time that Capo dressed in all black was when he was about to get his hands dirty. He walked up to me and gave me a quick peck on the lips before going over to the twins and doing the same thing.

"Be safe," I called out as he made his way out of the door. I sat at the kitchen table and put my head in my hands. I felt overwhelmed. I know I was supposed to think the best but I couldn't help thinking the opposite. I just got Capo back and it felt like I was going to lose him again. I couldn't picture my life without him.

I felt tiny hands on my leg and looked down to see Ja'kiyra had crawled over to me. No matter what I went through, my kids always made me smile. They were so innocent and I planned on keeping them that way. I picked her up and hugged her tightly. I never wanted my daughter to go through anything that I went through growing up. Although my past made me a stronger person, nobody should have to experience it.

I needed to get out of the house. I would drive myself crazy waiting for Capo to call and fill me in on what was going on so I walked over to wake up Janiylah. I figured I would take the kids out for ice cream or something. Janiylah stood up to stretch as I placed Ja'kiyra on the floor then proceeded to grab her and her brother's jackets.

The house phone began to ring, interrupting me from what I was doing but I quickly answered it.

"Hello," I said out of breath.

"Nae," it was Capo. "Have you heard from Boog?"

Instantly, I became nervous.

"No, why?"

"I called him but I didn't get an answer. I'll just try again later."

"Ja'kahri, what's going on?" I asked before he hung up. I was tired of being left in the dark and the fact that my brother was involved didn't sit well with me. "Does it have something to do wi-."

"Nae, I'll call you later," he cut me off then hung up. He knew that I hated being hung up on. I rolled my eyes and went back to getting the kids ready for the park. Janiylah had baby Kahri's jacket on and was finishing putting on Ja'kiyra's. I was grateful for Janiylah, she helped me out in more ways than one.

"Thanks, Niy," I said as I headed to the kitchen to pack a small bag for the kids drinks and snacks. Ten minutes later, we were ready to go. While putting the kid's stuff into the car, Janiylah broke my train of thought.

"Nae, what are you doing for the twins birthday?" she asked.

I froze, here it was the end of August and I hadn't even begun to plan the twin's first birthday bash.

"Damn," I said under my breath. "I hadn't even thought about it Niy. I'll start looking into stuff tonight."

Lately, my mind had been in other places especially with everything that was going on. I found myself doing random stuff just to keep my mind busy and off the bullshit .

"I'll help you out if you'd like," she offered. I smiled at her.

"That would be nice. Come on, we are going to the park for a little." I said carrying one baby while Janiylah carried the other. I locked the front door before jumping in the car so we could enjoy our day.

Chapter Two

Boog

Riding around the city while blowing down on this blunt, my mind was racing a mile a minute. I knew I fucked up major. I slipped up once and it could cost me everything I worked hard to hold together. I had a good woman in Michelle, yet my dog ass ways were still lingering around. Michelle was everything a nigga could ever ask for but I just couldn't let the past stay where it belonged. I had to go back, just one more time and that one time could possibly ruin everything.

I won't even lie; I wouldn't be surprised if Chelle decided she didn't want to fuck with a nigga anymore. It would kill me because I truly loved the girl, but to say I didn't know this shit would happen; I'd be lying out my ass. I told her in the beginning, I would try to do right by her and I swear on everything; I kept that promise.

However, one drunken night changed all that.

When Chelle and I became official, I swore off all my previous chicks, Kitty included. Kitty didn't understand the sudden change in me because one day we were fucking and the next day I was cutting her off. She told me, I was making a mistake by trying to settle down with one chick when I was used to fucking who ever I wanted, whenever I wanted.

Don't get it twisted though, I'm not a male hoe. I just had a select few ladies that I fucked with; they held me down during my three-year bid. I had to respect them, but a nigga's heart belonged to Michelle. I wanted to wrap my hands around Kitty's neck after the bullshit she pulled. Now Michelle was barely speaking to me and the shit was killing me.

I pulled up onto the block to see if any one of my niggas were out there that I could kick it with. I usually spoke to my sister, however I know she wouldn't do shit except tell me how wrong I am. I was wrong but I didn't need to be constantly reminded of it. I saw my nigga, Knuck standing on the block chopping it up with a few niggas. He recognized my car off rip.

"What's good nigga?" he said dapping me up after I rolled the window down.

"Shit man, a nigga is stressing."

"Hold on."

He walked back over to the niggas he was chopping it up with, dapped them up before making his way back to my ride. He hopped in and I pulled off. I relit the blunt that I had and focused on the road.

"What's the deal, Boog?"

"Man, I fucked up."

"How?"

I sighed, "Remember the last time I talked to you, I was telling you how I was sticking to one shortie and one shortie only? Well that shit was all good, but a nigga slipped up one time and it may haunt me for life."

"Fuck you talking about bruh?" Knuck asked, confused.

"Kitty is knocked up."

"What?!" he said, looking at me wide eyed.

"I don't know how the fuck this happened. I mean, I know how it happened but damn this is not what the fuck I need."

"Damn nigga."

"That ain't even the half of it nigga. Michelle's pregnant too."

"Damn, you've been a busy little nigga, huh?" Knuck laughed.

"My nigga if I felt this was funny, I'd laugh with you. Kitty showed up at my crib, telling my girl some shit. I swear on my mama, if I could, I'd whoop Kitty's ass but I don't have time to be doing anymore bids."

"Nah, I feel you my nigga. So what you going to do?"

I sighed because that question has been wracking my brain for the last two weeks. "Man, I don't even know. I do know that I need this shit handled. I can't lose my shortie behind some bullshit."

I turned back onto the block because I knew that's where Knuck wanted to be. He always made time for a nigga even if it was just to vent.

"Whatever you do homie, you know I got your back no matter what. Just let me know what you need a nigga for," he said dapping me up.

"I got you homie, and I appreciate you taking this ride with me."

"Never an issue, my nigga. You know we go way back." We dapped each other up again and he climbed out my car. I needed to talk to Michelle to see where her head was. If she was trying to leave a nigga, then I'd rather know now. I don't need any surprises coming up during another argument.

Chapter Three

Michelle

Every time I looked at Boog, I wanted to slap the shit out of him. The day I opened the door and saw that bitch standing there, made me want to fuck her up but I had to think about my unborn seed. I didn't plan on telling Boog about the baby the way I did, but I definitely couldn't let that bitch think she was the only one. I was prepared to handle shit on my own if need be, although I really didn't want to.

I had been giving him the silent treatment because I had nothing to say to him. What could I possibly have said? He shouldn't have been out fucking the next bitch anyway. I loved his ass to death, but nah I would not be putting up with his bullshit or the bitches he wants to fuck. Don't get me wrong, I know dealing with a street nigga, bitches come with the territory but I wasn't for it. And I definitely didn't want that shit brought to my door.

I just finished a therapeutic shopping trip. I knew it wasn't needed, but hell why not blow the nigga's money. Shopping kept my mind off of not crying. Everything in me wanted to break down and cry but it wouldn't solve anything or change the fact that the bitch may be pregnant, by my man.

"Ugh," I said out loud.

I headed towards the parking garage, where my car was to load the bags in. It was a quarter to one and I had a doctor's appointment at one fifteen. I thought about telling Boog about the appointment, but I didn't want him thinking that was an open invitation for him to talk to me. I still had nothing to say, so I would just show him the paperwork later and deal with his shit talking. I backed out of the parking spot, but it was short lived by a car honking at me.

"Watch where you're going," the driver yelled.

I could have sworn I checked all my mirrors, but I quickly apologized before putting my car in drive to pull off.

"Aye," he yelled causing me to stop again. I looked through my rearview mirror and noticed him getting out of his car before making his way towards my window. I cracked the window as he bent down to look at me.

"Can I get your name?"

"Chelle."

"Chelle what?"

"Just Chelle."

"Okay, just Chelle. I'm Tyson, Tyson Miller. Do you think we can exchange numbers?"

I quickly thought about it, as mad as I was at Boog, I

wouldn't do the same shit he did to me.

"I have a man," I said as I began rolling the window back up.

"Wait."

I rolled my eyes. *This nigga is persistent.*

"You can take my number and whenever you're ready, you call me." Once I registered his voice, I realized it sounded familiar. I looked at him again and tried to remember where I knew him from.

"Wait, don't I know you?"

"Nah, but I'm trying to get to know you," he said, still trying to spit game.

"Nah, I know you from somewhere. You have a nickname?"

"Trouble."

I snapped my finger. "Yep, you used to try to talk to my girl."

"Who is your girl?"

"Jonnae."

I saw his face flush before the look of anger fell across it.

"Oh, her."

"Yeah, her. Now I gotta go," I said, rolling up my window and pulling off. Wait until I tell Jonnae about this shit. From the look on his face, it's almost like he had a bad taste in his mouth at the mention of her name. I couldn't wait to get home and talk to her about it. But for now, let me hurry and make it to this appointment, since he already held me up longer than I had the time for.

Chapter Four

Jarell

"*I need you Jarell, and our daughter needs you.*" I can still hear Alicia's voice clear on my voicemail. Daughter? Fuck is she talking about my daughter needs me? I don't have a daughter. Alicia always had been on that bullshit. This was part of the reason, I stopped fucking with her. She never knew when to be serious; when we were together she thought everything was a joke. She always did extra shit to get my attention and I wasn't with that shit right now.

"Lemme call this chick back and see what the fuck she's talking about," I said out loud. I didn't need things being ruined with Jass over some bullshit. I dialed her number and jumped in my truck, headed to the crib. I was tired as fuck and ready to take a nap.

"About time you returned my call," Alicia said answering the phone.

"Man I don't got time for the bullshit. What is this shit you talking about, with my daughter? I don't have a daughter." I got straight to the point, fuck playing around and talking in circles.

"You do have a daughter Jarell, she's almost two." She was damn near whispering.

"What the fuck you mean; I have a daughter who's almost two? Alicia quit with the bullshit, yo."

"I'm not bullshitting you Jarell. Her name is Jaynell, and she'll be two on September 10th. She looks just like you, has your dimples and everything."

I pulled into the driveway of my house, killed the engine and took a deep breath.

"Why the fuck would you wait two years to tell me some shit like this? I missed everything Alicia! EVERY FUCKING THING! Even if she is my child, I can't get any of that time I lost back." I wasn't even sure if this kid was mine and the shit had my blood boiling.

"I'm sorry. I can't change shit no matter how bad I wish I could, but now, I'm telling you that she needs you. If you want to hate me for the rest of your life, that's fine with me, but don't take it out on your daughter. She's innocent."

I sighed, "I want a test Alicia. I can't just take your word for it. You don't just spring shit like this on a nigga like it's all good. She's fucking two years old!"

"I know Rell, trust me. I look at her every day and all I see is you. I never wanted it to be like this. I was doing fine taking care of her by myself, but shit is getting too hot and too fast. I got to protect my daughter before anything. If a test is what you want, you'll get it, but only if you promise me something," she stated.

"What?"

"You'll take care of her, once you find out she is your daughter." I didn't like the sound in her voice, but I didn't want to get into it over the phone.

"Of course Alicia, you know me better than that."

"That's all I ask," and with that, she hung up.

I sat in my truck for another five minutes before getting out and heading into the crib. I dropped my keys on the table and headed upstairs to the bathroom. The events of the last twenty-four hours were a bit much. First the shit with Capo and that bum ass nigga Chink, to finding out I could possibly have a daughter. The bad part about it was, I hadn't fucked with Alicia in over three years. We called it quits and the next thing I know, she just up and left. I was a young nigga, but that shit fucked me up.

I released my bladder then grabbed some bud and a dutch off my dresser. I needed to get high and quick.

How the fuck do I tell Jasmine that I possibly have a child? I thought to myself. That shit was still blowing my mind. I missed shit I wouldn't ever be able to see happen. The thought of her being my daughter and Alicia causing me to miss it all, pissed me off all over again.

My phone rang, breaking me from my thoughts. Looking at the phone, Capo's name flashed across the screen.

"What's good bruh?" I answered.

"Where you at nigga?"

I could hear the wind whipping in the background so either he was standing outside or in the car driving with the windows open.

"At the crib."

"For the head?" he questioned.

"Yeah."

"Aight, call Boog. I'm about to swing through. We have an issue play boy."

"Say no more."

We ended the call. I wondered what was going on. Capo wasn't one to talk much over the phone; he would hang up on a person before getting into detail. I dialed Boog's number.

"Yo," he answered.

"Aye, come to my crib. Cap is on his way here too."

"Yup." He hung up, without saying another word. I finished rolling my blunt and instantly sparked it. Once again, I was lost in my thoughts.

Thirty minutes later, both Capo and Boog were pulling up to my house at the same time. I opened the door, eating a bag of chips. I was munched out like a motherfucka.

I dapped up both of them as Boog shut the door behind him and we headed to the kitchen. Capo and Boog took a seat.

"What's the deal?"

Capo sighed as he looked back and forth between Boog and myself.

"Which one of you didn't call the clean up crew after we left that bitch ass nigga's house?"

My high was instantly blown.

Oh shit. We fucked up now.

Chapter Five

Alicia

I looked at my daughter while she slept. She reminded me so much of Jarell. Daily, it bugged me that he wasn't around, but I couldn't blame anybody but myself. The moment my mother found out I was pregnant, she shipped me off to live with my father, three hours away in Stamford, Connecticut. He wanted me to have an abortion, but I fought against it. Although I was sixteen when I got pregnant and seventeen when I had her, she was mine; a piece of me and I refused to get rid of her.

I sighed deeply. Here I was almost three years later, caught up in more shit than I should have been. I put my life in danger and with my life being in danger; it meant that my daughter's life was in danger a well. I regretted the choices I made with every bone in my body.

I know you're wondering what happened and how I

ended up in such a fucked up situation that has me calling Jarell after all these years.

I moved out of my father's house after I had Jaynell. He and his wife were trying to run my every move and I wasn't having it. I begun working right away when I got to Connecticut, finished high school and saved my money. I had a small baby shower because my father and his wife bought everything else for the baby. When Jaynell was three months, I moved out on my own and haven't looked back.

I started dating Monroe when Jaynell was ten months. Everything was cool in the beginning, he spoiled the shit out of Jaynell and me. I started stacking my money and allowing him to spend his on us. He got locked up three weeks after Jaynell's first birthday. I wrote letters, came to visit as much as I could and put money in his account. Monroe left us money, but I used that mainly for his account.

During a   trip to see him two weeks ago, he asked me to pick up some money from one of his boys and meet up with his connect to pay him. Simple right? I said the same thing. Everything was squared away. I picked up the money and left it in my trunk so that I could meet with the connect early in the morning to do the drop. I didn't want any dealings around Jaynell.

I woke up the following morning to find the trunk of my car popped and the black duffle bag gone. I felt like the wind was knocked out of me. Just that easy, twenty-five stacks was gone. It blew my mind because I lived in a pretty quiet neighborhood. I instantly told Monroe what happened when he called and he flipped out. He made it seem as though it was my fault and said he would take care of it.

I thought he did until I received a call the following day that my days were numbered. I had to get my daughter away from harm, away from here, and away from me.

Chapter Six

Capo

I looked back and forth between Boog and Jarell, waiting for one of them to answer me. I refused to go down for somebody else's mistake, so one of them better speak up and soon.

"Hello!" I said breaking the silence.

"ManI know for a fact, I called Chauncey and them to come clean that shit up," Boog said. "I couldn't stay around to wait but I told them how to get in and where it was."

"So nobody waited to see if these niggas showed up?"

"Nah, I ain't even gonna lie; I dipped shortly after you did," Rell said. I shook my head. If I could have slapped the shit out of both of them, I would have. These two dumb motherfuckas were not about to cost me my fucking freedom.

"Somebody get Chauncey's ass on the phone," I

snapped. Before anybody could move, I heard the front door open.

"Babe?" I heard Jass call out.

"Yeah?" Rell responded.

"Where are you?"

"Kitchen." She walked in and looked at us. I knew with me being dressed in all black in August wasn't normal so she instantly got a nervous look.

"Everything okay?" she asked.

"Yeah," I answered. "Both of y'all meet me in an hour at the crib," I told them. I didn't say anything else as I walked out of the door. My mind was racing a mile a minute. I needed to holla at this nigga Chauncey and quick. I pulled out my phone and dialed his number.

"Yo," he answered.

"Where you at?"

"West End. Why what's good?"

"Meet me at the field. I got to holla at you," I told him. I hung up because I knew his ass was gonna ask me questions that I really wasn't in the mood to answer over the phone. I double-checked to make sure my gun was still on my hip. As I took the long way to the field on the West End, I reflected on some shit.

I needed change. I had two kids to live for as well as my sister and brother. When I first got with Jonnae, I was trying to transition out of the streets. Yes, I was young but I had to provide for my siblings. Unfortunately, Jarell was trying to follow in my footsteps. Although I didn't want him in the streets, I would rather him work with me than with someone else. Now, here I was back in some street shit with not only my little brother but my girl's brother too. A part of me was kicking myself in the ass for getting them involved. Boog was a street dude, so I knew he was used to this shit. I hoped Jarell would see that this wasn't for him, and turn away.

My phone rang just as I pulled into the parking lot. I noticed it was my brother.

"Yo."

"Aye. Where you at?"

"Handling business. What's up?" I spotted Chauncey sitting on the bleachers.

"I need to holla at you about some personal shit," he said.

"A'ight. I'll be home in like thirty minutes. Meet me there."

"Cool."

We hung up and I climbed out of the car.

"So," I said walking up behind him. "did you not get the call the other day for a job on Miller Ave?" I asked him.

"Yeah, why?"

"You received the payment for that job too, right?"

"Yeah."

"So, do you want to tell me why the fucking body was still in the fucking house and probably heading to the morgue, right now? Do you not get paid to dispose of shit like that?"

"Cap, I can explain."

"What the fuck can you explain?"

"I pulled up to the crib and there was somebody on the porch. I meant to go back but I forgot," he said.

"You forgot? You forgot?" I asked him as my voice elevated. "How the fuck do you forget to do something, I fuckin' paid you to do?" I became even more pissed as I thought about how I called, another one of my youngin's to drop the money off to this nigga baby mama. "Your ass didn't forget to take my fuckin' money though. I'll tell you what; either you repay me my money and take this rap since you want to fuckin' forget. Or your family will be making funeral arrangements for you, your baby mama and your kids," I told him. Little did he know, I would never harm any kid. I would definitely make them fatherless though. I had no problem doing that. "Forty-eight hours, nigga."

I walked back to my car and pulled off. I didn't plan on jeopardizing my freedom but as a man, I had to do what I had to do.

Chapter Seven

Jonnae

I couldn't help but to smile, as I looked at my kids' faces as me and Janiylah pushed them in the swings. On the outside I was smiling but on the inside, I was scared shitless. I lost Ja'kahri once for a month for some bullshit and now it looked as if he was wrapped up in more shit. The first time, I was behind him because I knew he was innocent. But based off the way he dashed out of the house earlier, I knew the shit at Erick's house had Ja'kahri Amir Turner's name written all over it.

"You okay?" Janiylah asked me breaking my train of thought.

"Yeah," I sighed. "I was just thinking about a few things."

She didn't say anything else as she kept pushing Kahri. My phone began vibrating in my pocket. Pulling it out, I noticed an unfamiliar number calling.

"Hello," I answered suspiciously.

"Jonnae?" I instantly recognized the voice as Chink's mother.

"Yes. How are you Mrs. Jackson?"

"Not good, honey. Not good at all." I could hear the pain in her voice and automatically knew why she was calling. "Do you think we can meet up?"

"Uh, I should have some time. Let me get back to you later with a definite answer though."

"Okay."

I hung up the phone and my mind drifted off again. I wondered why the hell she wanted to meet up with me . I quickly dialed Capo's number.

"Yeah, Nae."

"Where are you?"

"Heading to the house to meet Rell. What's up?"

"Okay, I'll meet you there. I have something to tell you."

"A'ight."

We ended our call and I pulled Kiyra out of the swing.

"Come on," I said. "Let's go see daddy." Janiylah grabbed Kahri and we left. My mind was all over the place with why Chink's mother could be calling me. I hadn't spoken to her since Chink and I split up. The ride home was quiet and luckily the twins had fallen asleep. Within fifteen minutes, we were home. I was glad that Jarell hadn't made it there yet.

"Niy, can you help me lay them in their room?"

She nodded and climbed out.

"Babe?" I called as we walked inside the house.

"Yeah," he answered as he came down the stairs. He grabbed Kahri from Janiylah and headed back upstairs to their room. I followed him and closed the door behind us when we got there.

"Erick's mother called me," I told him.

"Saying what?"

"She said she want to meet with me. I don't know for what though."

"What did you tell her?"

"I told her I would let her know. Honestly, I wanna know what she wants to talk about."

"Why?"

I could tell he was getting upset.

"Because what if she knows something? I would rather know ahead of time before shit blows up. I don't know about you but I give a shit about this family," I snapped. I sometimes hated Capo's nonchalant attitude about shit. I had a bad feeling someone close to me was going to be pulled in this shit.

"She doesn't know shit and you know it."

"I don't know what she knows. I do know that he and his mother were close so I wouldn't be surprised if she knows something about the recent activities. Like I said, I care about this family and I'll do whatever to protect it."

I left him standing in the kid's room by himself. I went back downstairs and found Janiylah in the kitchen, making a sandwich.

"Niy, I have to head out. If your brother leaves, call me. The kids are still sleeping."

She nodded as she stuffed part of her sandwich in her mouth. I grabbed my keys and headed out the door. As I got to the car, I pulled out my phone and called the number that Chink's mother called from.

"Hello?" she answered.

"Hey. Where did you want to meet at?"

I heard her sniffle on the other end.

"How does Newport Creamery sound?" she asked.

"That's fine. I'll be there in about ten minutes."

"Okay," she replied and hung up.

I jumped on Rte. 10 and headed there as my mind wandered. Here I was almost twenty-one, a mother of twins and I had a fiancé who seemed as though he couldn't get enough of the streets. I shook my head as I got off of the Dean St. exit. At that moment, I realized I had to get myself together for my children and Janiylah. She needed an positive female role model in her life.

I pulled into the parking lot and called Erick's mother to let her know I was outside. I found a spot as I told her what kind of car I had and where I was parked. I watched her head over to my car. The moment she climbed in, I took took one look at her and knew she had been crying nonstop. I felt bad for her; well to an extent. Her son had caused so much drama and turmoil in my life, but no parent should have to bury their child.

"Hey," she said just above a whisper. "Thank you for coming to meet with me. I appreciate it."

"No problem."

"You were with my son for a few years. I knew when you guys split he was hurt. But why did you guys split? Erick never told me."

I sighed. The last thing I wanted to do was relive my life with Chink.

"I walked in on him and my ex best friend having sex."
She gasped.

"He seemed to always have trouble keeping his member in his pants," I continued. I know the last thing she wanted was to hear about her son's sex life but she asked.

"Wow. Well okay. He never told me that. If nothing else, you knew Erick and I were very close. I'm not sure if you heard when he was shot in the knee."

Whether he had told me, or Capo told me; I knew. There was no way I didn't.

"I heard about it," I told her.

"Have you ever heard of a guy named Cap, Capo, or something like that?"

My heart instantly started racing. I wanted to verbally answer but I knew my voice would be shaky as hell. I shook my head instead.

"Hm, ya know, I've known you probably close to seven years. This is the first time you've ever looked me directly in my face and lied. I had a lot of respect for you, Jonnae, up until this very moment. Again, you know my son and me were close so you know, he told me who shot him. He even mentioned your brother being there."

"Listen," I stopped her. "With all due respect, but I don't involve myself in my brother's mess."

"But what about the father of your kids?"

"What about him?"

"I know he was the one who shot my baby. I wouldn't be surprised if he had something to do with his death."

"That's where I draw the line," I snapped. "You're not going to sit in my face and disrespect my family based off of some whack ass assumptions. Your son was not perfect by any means. Did he ever tell you that he beat some girl's ass and placed the blame on somebody else? Your son had him in jail for some shit he didn't even do. You've sat in my face, did nothing but speculate and spew a bunch of bullshit. Now, I'm sorry you have to bury your son but you need to go. Lose my number."

She opened the car door and looked back at me before speaking.

"I heard your children are beautiful. I would hate for something to happen to them."

"I will die before I allow anyone to cause them harm. Get the fuck out of my car."

"I will get justice for my son, even if that means tearing your little family apart." She climbed out and slammed the door behind her. I quickly backed out and pulled off. I couldn't wait to tell Capo this shit.

Chapter Eight

Boog

I just got to Capo's house and watched as he pulled into his driveway. This shit with Erick had my mind fucked up. Add to that, the fact that Michelle sent me pictures of her sonogram from her doctor's appointment, had me ready to bust a cap in somebody's ass. I'm not sure what kind of shit Chelle called herself pulling by not letting me know about her fucking doctor's appointment, but she picked the right one to play with. Sending me a picture message of a damn sonogram of my baby pissed me off. I didn't give a fuck how much shit me and Michelle were going through, I wanted to be there from beginning until the very end of her pregnancy. Missing appointments was something I couldn't get back.

"You cool homie?" Capo asked me bringing me out of my daze.

"Yeah bruh, I'm alright. Aye, lemme ask you something."

"Shoot."

"How was Nae during her pregnancy?"

"Emotional as fuck. Sometimes I wanted to yell and tell her to shut the fuck up, but then I had to remember her hormones were all over the place."

I knew exactly how he felt because sometimes Chelle's ass would start crying out the blue.

"Why you ask?"

"I'm just wondering if pregnancy would make her do some dumb shit that she normally wouldn't do."

"Oh yeah, for sure. I caught her ass in the mall with some nigga. Granted I was with Lani but I damn sure didn't expect to turn around to see Nae walking and laughing with some random nigga. That shit definitely pissed me off," Capo explained.

"Chelle had an appointment today and she didn't tell me but decided she wanted to send me a picture of a fucking sonogram. Tell me where the fuck do they do that at? I swear that shit got me wanting to choke the shit out of her."

"Now Nae hasn't ever pulled no foul shit like that, but at the same time my nigga look at what y'all are going through? How do you expect her to handle the fact that you may have a shortie on the way with someone else?"

"Man, I know that, but when she decided to stay, I figured she forgave me. I didn't think I would still be fucking paying for this shit. I'm not saying what I did was right because in no way, shape or form was it."

Capo just sat back. I often came to him for advice about this pregnancy shit because he dealt with this already. This shit would make a nigga want to stay the fuck away. Women either cried or were needy as fuck.

"In all honesty bruh, you got to take that shit day by day or that shit will have you going crazy. Remember, if she wasn't pregnant, she would be your sassy little shortie that you're used to," he said as he mashed the roach of the blunt out. I stood up from the patio seat I was sitting in and prepared to leave. I couldn't deal with this shit right now.

"Aight my nigga, I'll holla at you later. Tell Nae to call me. Let me know what you want to do about this shit with that nigga too," I told him.

"I got you."

I made my way out the door, jumped in the car and headed home. I was glad I smoked that blunt to mellow out because I wanted to wring Michelle's neck. As I pulled into the driveway of the condo, I saw Michelle's Infiniti outside. I took a deep breath and headed inside.

"Michelle?" I called.

"What," she said coming out of the kitchen, eating a bag of Sour Cream and Onion potato chips.

"So you want to explain why you didn't feel the need to tell me you had an appointment today?" I asked her.

"Because any other time I call you, you don't answer. I wasn't going to waste my time. Plus, I told you beforehand. I reminded you two days ago; if your memory is that bad then you need to leave that weed alone."

I sucked my teeth, "Now all of a sudden the weed is an issue? Man, get the fuck outta here with that bullshit. I want to know why you didn't feel the need to at least shoot a nigga a text."

"I didn't know what or *who* you were doing so I didn't,"

she said making sure to put emphasis on the who.

"Lemme ask you something," I said leaning against the counter as she sat at the kitchen island.

"What's that?" she asked, popping another chip into her mouth.

"If you're constantly gonna bring up the other bitches and the baby comment all the time, what the fuck was the point in you remaining here? I'm not asking you to forget what the fuck happened but I damn sure don't need you throwing that shit in my fucking face."

"How the fuck do you expect me to feel Jonathan? I took a chance on you and you let me down. I cared when it seemed like the rest of the world was against you. I've remained by your side through all the bullshit since we've been together and not once did I complain. Next thing I know, there's a bitch at my door talking about she's pregnant by my dude and you want me to sweep it under the rug like it's nothing? I'm sorry, that's not going to happen," she cried.

"Man, quit all that fucking crying. I didn't even say or do anything to you and you sitting there fucking crying."

"You are so fucking insensitive! Let me go fuck the next nigga and have him show up at your house, talking about he knocked me up. You'll be ready to paint these fucking streets red," she said. She was right. Let a nigga approach me in any way about my girl and it was on before he could even realize it.

"She didn't show up at your house, she showed up at mine."

I have no idea where the fuck that came from but I knew it came out all fucking wrong.

"Your house? Okay, cool, say no more. We're out," she said as she stood up to leave.

"Baby wait," I tried stopping her.

She pulled away, grabbed her handbag off the couch and was out the door. I slumped on the couch with my head thrown back. *Maybe this relationship shit ain't for a nigga like me* I thought to myself as I closed my eyes and drifted off.

Chapter Nine

Michelle

I honestly had no idea what Jonathan was going through but I needed him to get his shit together. I was gonna prove to his ass that I didn't need him. I loved him yes, but to hell with him, getting his ass on his back and taking it out on me. If he has a baby by this bitch then so be it; my child and I would be perfectly fine.

Thirty minutes later, I pulled up to my mother's house. I always found my way back to my mama whenever I needed someone to talk to.

"Mama," I yelled, while walking through the front door.

"Hey Meeshy," she said, coming into the living room. "What brings you by here today?"

I sighed, "I just needed to get away."

"Meeshy, you're my daughter, so I know you. You never show up at my house for no reason, so talk to your mom."

I broke down and told my mother about everything that had been going on between Boog and I. To say she was surprised would be an understatement.

"Why the hell have you not said anything before?"

"Ma, I don't want to bring my relationship drama to you. It's not your issue, it's mine."

"Um, you're my child so any problem you have, is mine. I don't need you stressing out my grandbaby either."

I looked at her like she was crazy. *How the fuck does she know? I haven't even told her* I thought to myself.

"You're my only child and my daughter. You don't think I didn't notice your hips spreading? The only way hips spread like that is if there is a bun in the oven. So tell me, how far along you are and when your due date is."

I was too shocked to say anything. My voice was stuck. "Uh, um, I'm seven weeks."

She smiled and pulled me into a hug. I wrapped my arms tightly around her and for a second, it seemed as if every bad feeling I had, had gone out of the window. It doesn't matter how old I got, my mother would always be my best friend.

"Okay, enough of this mushy stuff," she said breaking from the hug. "You hungry?"

"What you cooking?"

"What is it you want?"

I sat and thought about it for a minute. I loved my mama's cooking, period.

"How about some chicken with mac and cheese and string beans?" My stomach began growling just thinking about the food. My mama could cook her ass off. It had been a while since I last had her food.

"Coming right up."

I watched as my mama began moving around the kitchen. I then turned and looked around the living room at the home I grew up in. There were pictures lining the walls of me showing my growth through the years. I was an only child. Growing up, I wanted a sibling but my parents never made it happen.

"Meeshy, your father should be on his way. I know he would be happy to see you. It's been a while since you decided to show your face," my mom said.

I rolled my eyes for several reasons. One, my father wasn't a fan of my relationship with Boog, and he made sure to let me know about it every time he spoke to me. And two, my mama's sarcasm wasn't needed at all. My father had my number just as I had his. If he wanted to talk to me, he could call.

"I guess," I mumbled then tossed myself on the couch, snatching the remote off the living room table. I flipped through the channels until I came across the First 48. I grabbed my phone, out of my back pocket and checked to see if Boog tried to reach out but he hadn't. That had me feeling some type of way, but I wasn't going to reach out to him first.

An hour later, almost like clock work, my mama finished cooking and my father walked in the door.

"Hey honey, dinner just finished up, wash your hands and come eat," my mother greeted my father while I rolled my eyes.

"Michelle," he spoke. I looked up and noticed him standing on the side of the couch I was sitting on.

"Hi." I looked back at the television. He stood there, staring at me for a few minutes before walking away, to get ready to eat. I won't lie; it kind of bothered me that my father and I had such a strained relationship.

Growing up, I was the biggest daddy's girl ever. My father spoiled me rotten and I loved him more than I could ever put into words. Our relationship was always good. That was until I started dealing with Boog. He didn't see Boog as much more than a thug that his daughter was too good for. I tried to explain to him that Boog was good guy and meant well numerous times but he was convinced he was nothing but a 'low-life'.

I would always love my father but his attitude could be kept to himself. I could love him from a distance. I couldn't help who I fell in love with. It's not like Boog changed my life for the worse. Just like every other relationship, we had problems, but that didn't make him the worse person ever. If my dad found out about the shit going on now, it would only confirm his thoughts even more.

I pushed the situation with Boog and the ill feelings towards my father to the back of my mind as I headed into the kitchen to have a dinner with my parents; something I hadn't done in a long time.

Chapter Ten

Jarell

I tried to hide the fact that something was bothering me from Jass. I didn't want her to start asking questions because truth be told, I didn't know how to go about answering them just yet. I knew how much Jass loved me, but I didn't know if it was enough to accept my child. Yes, she was from a previous relationship and I knew nothing about her, but it didn't stop the fact that she could be mine. If she was, then there was no doubt I would take care of her.

"Ma, I'll be back," I said as I walked out of the door without giving her a chance to answer. I needed to talk to my brother and quick. I jumped in my car to go to Capo and Nae's crib. It was times like this, I wish my mother was still alive. She would have got in Alicia's ass and she would tell me how to handle the situation. I sighed as I turned into Capo's driveway ten minutes later. I beeped the horn twice before killing the engine and stepping out.

Janiylah opened the door with a big smile on her face.

"Rell!"

"What's up, sis?" I pulled her into my embrace and squeezed her. I loved my sister to death and I thanked God daily for blessing us with her. I may not be the best big brother, but for my sister, I would die. "Where's Cap at?"

"He just came in not too long ago so he's somewhere around here." I walked inside the house and she closed the door behind me. "Check the basement or backyard," she said before walking off towards the living room. I walked over to the basement door, opened it and noticed that the lights were off so I figured he was outside. As I reached the back door, I could smell weed so I knew he was out there and smoking.

"Yo," I spoke up making presence known. "What's going on?" I walked up behind him then stood off to the side.

"Shit man, just thinking about everything that's been going on."

"You think that's bad? Listen to this shit. You remember the little bad bitch Alicia I used to fuck with a couple of years back?" He nodded as he inhaled more smoke.

"What about her?"

"Tell me why she called me talking about I have a daughter."

Capo started choking uncontrollably. I patted his back until he got it under control.

"Say what?"

I pulled out my phone and replayed the voicemail for him. He listened intently.

"The fuck is wrong with this broad? Have you called her?"

"Yeah, I called her back. She said she got into some shit and needed me to take the little girl. If she's mine, I don't mind taking her; but I don't appreciate her waiting over three years to tell me this shit. I missed everything that this little girl has gone through, including her birth."

"Shit like that would cause me to want to slap the shit out of her. I wish Jonnae would try some shit like that, I would shove my foot in her ass," he said seriously. I chuckled at him. I then took a deep breath and sighed.

"I don't know what to do bruh. I mean, of course I want to know if she's really mine, but then what about Jass? She doesn't deserve this shit. I don't even know if she'll stay with a nigga after this shit."

"Jass can't be mad because it's not like you hid it from her or you cheated on her. I mean don't get me wrong, it's a tough situation regardless, but I can't see her getting too upset about it."

"Bruh! You know Jass and she don't take no shit. To be honest, I think she's going to leave me."

"I hope not," he said as he passed me the blunt. I took it and inhaled.

"I hope not either."

"You taking a test?" he asked me.

"No doubt. I'm not doing shit until I find out if she's mine or not."

"When are you supposed to do that?"

"Shit I don't even know. Let me call her and ask when

she plans on doing this. I need this done ASAP." He nodded as I tapped on Alicia's number and placed the phone to my ear.

"Hello," she answered on the second ring.

"Yo, when do you plan on doing this test and shit?"

"The sooner the better. I can come down there within the next two days," she said. I thought about it. With today being Saturday, a testing center probably wouldn't be open until Monday.

"Come down Monday and we can get it handled."

"Okay." She hung up before I could say anything else. Capo and I were silent as we finished smoking the blunt.

"If the test says she is your child, what you plan on doing ?"

"Man I'm going to have to do the right thing for my kid. I don't know what Alicia got herself caught up in, but it must be serious if she wants her daughter with me instead.."

Capo nodded in agreement.

"You know whatever you choose, I got you," he assured me. I reached out my hand to dap him up.

"I appreciate it."

Chapter Eleven

Alicia

I was glad that Jarell was willing to do the test, although I knew once he took one look at Jaynell, he would know that she was his. I hated that they had to meet under these circumstances though. As I stared at her, I was regretting keeping her from her father . She deserved better but I gave her everything I ever wanted her to have. I hated that I would end up missing out on the rest of her life but I knew Jarell would take good care of her. I loved my daughter enough to protect her, even if it meant I wouldn't see her again.

The thought alone caused me to cry. I never imagined getting myself caught up in some shit like this. I thought I had it all figured out but God was quick to show me that the hustler's life was more than I bargained for. I regretted even agreeing to do the shit.

I had yet to hear from Monroe since then. I tried to visit him but he would deny my visits. I even called the jail and asked that they have him call me ASAP but he never did. I felt as though he left me out high and dry. I had nowhere to turn. I knew I couldn't go running back to my father because I knew he wouldn't listen to shit I had to say. I had been cooped up in my house only going out when needed. I hated looking over my shoulder every step I took. I knew Jaynell was tired of it because all she did was whine. Once Jaynell was away from harm, I would be willing to accept my punishment with no regrets.

I looked back at my daughter as she slept. I was up early, getting ready to head back to Rhode Island. I hadn't been there since I left almost four years ago. I hadn't even spoken to my mother since the day she shipped me off to my father. She tried reaching out a few times, but I wasn't for it. If she really cared about me, she would have let me stay to guide me, instead she took the easy route and shipped me off. Fuck her.

I quickly threw on some sweats and my shoes. I didn't bother to get Jaynell dressed because I didn't plan on waking her up. I packed her a little bag with her clothes in it and went outside to throw it in my trunk. I double-checked my surroundings before running from my car and back in the house. I hated living like this but I brought it upon myself. I scooped my daughter up and locked my front door before rushing outside to strap her in her car seat. I placed her neck pillow around her neck, so that she could sleep comfortably on our drive. I ran around to the driver's side of my car, started it up and pulled out of my driveway.

I jumped on 95N, heading towards Rhode Island. I continually glanced in my rearview mirror looking for any car that could be considered suspicious. My eyes began to water. If you would have asked me a year ago, if I would be in this position, I would have told you no. This was not the life I wanted to live.

Three and a half hours later, I saw the Welcome to Rhode Island sign. I dialed Jarell's number and asked him where he wanted to meet. He gave me the address and I punched it in my GPS. He told me what kind of car he would be in. Although the traffic through Connecticut was a little heavy, I was glad the Rhode Island traffic wasn't as bad.

I took the exit labeled Cranston and headed toward the DNA center at the Cranston ACI. Five minutes later, I dialed Jarell's number and told him I was down the street. Pulling into the parking lot, I spotted him standing on the side of a charcoal gray Mercedes Benz. I pulled into an empty spot three cars down before taking a deep breath, killing the engine and stepping out.

It had been so long since I saw Jarell, yet I still got butterflies when I was around him. My breath became caught in my throat as I came face to face with him. I couldn't do anything but stare.

"You can't speak?" he asked. I shook my head and smiled.

"I'm sorry. You're still as handsome as you were the last time I saw you," I told him honestly.

"Who knows where we would be if you hadn't left."

"Jarell, my mother forced me," I told him as my voice

became shaky.

"You could have told me something, Lee," he said, calling me by the nickname he gave me years ago. I couldn't help but smile. "What happened? Why'd you leave?"

I sighed. "I found out I was pregnant. My mother wanted me to get rid of it. I refused so she sent me to live with my father, three hours away."

"Three hours away and you never bothered coming back at all? Besides that though, why didn't you tell me?"

I shrugged. "I knew you would be pissed that I left. I figured you would never want to hear from me again. I thought it was the right thing to do."

He shook his head. "Where is she?"

I walked around the passenger's side of the car and opened the back door. Jaynell was still sleeping. I leaned in and unbuckled her seatbelt. The moment I lifted her out of her seat, she woke up.

"Jarell, this is Jaynell."

Chapter Twelve

Jarell

My eyes locked on the little girl and it was as if I was staring into my mother's light brown eyes again. I almost lost my breath at the sight of her. *She's beautiful* I thought to myself.

"Hi pretty girl," I said. She smiled and that was all of the confirmation I needed. Besides the fact that she looked just like my family like Alicia said, she had my dimples and all. "If I give you another address, can you meet me there?"

"I thought we were getting the test done."

"I got all of the confirmation I need. Meet me at this address." I spit off the address to Capo's house. I took another look at the little girl before I walked off. The second I was in the car, I called my brother.

"Yo," he answered.

"Nigga I'm on my way to your house."

"A'ight, Nae and Niylah just left. The twins are down for a nap. Everything cool?"

"Man," I sighed. "Alicia came down so we can do that test."

"What happened?"

"I don't even need it," I told him, thinking about how much Alicia's daughter looked like me.

"Why not?"

"Nigga, you think the twins look like you? This little girl is a spitting image of me with Ma's eyes."

"Whoa."

"Exactly. Anyway, I told her to meet me at your house so you can see for yourself."

"A'ight. Let me know when you're outside."

"Cool." I ended my call with my brother and drove to his house in complete silence. I always wanted kids but I never thought my first one would be like this. I wanted to experience first everything's with my kids and now I would have to settle for being almost three years late. I shook my head at the thought. Alicia owed me a very long talk later but right now, I needed my brother's confirmation for what I already knew.

Thirteen minutes later, I pulled into Capo's driveway and rolled a blunt. For some reason, my nerves were bad. Having Alicia in my presence had caused some old feelings to rise. Feelings that I thought were long gone, resurfaced the moment she stepped out of her car.

Just as I lit the tip of the blunt, I spotted Alicia's car pulling into the driveway. I took a few pulls before putting it out. I left my windows cracked to air out my car as I climbed out and went to meet her.

"Who's house is this?" she asked as she walked around to grab our daughter out of the backseat.

Before I could answer, Jonnae pulled up behind Alicia's car. I could see the twisted look on her face. She quickly killed her engine and hopped out.

"Who the f…"

"Alicia?" Janiylah questioned as she closed the passenger's side door. My eyes bugged slightly because I was surprised Niylah remembered her.

"Wow. Janiylah, you've gotten big and matured into a beautiful young lady," Alicia said.

"Anybody want to tell me what is going on?" Jonnae snapped.

"Chill Nae, she's with me." I could see her face become calmer as she walked towards the house, I stayed back as Alicia grabbed our daughter out of the car. Janiylah watched and her mouth dropped the moment she saw Jaynell's face.

"Rell, she looks just like you," she said. I nodded and stared at the little girl. She looked around between me and Niylah before laying her head on her mother's shoulder.

"I know." I started walking towards the house. I could hear Jonnae flipping out and shook my head. Capo was walking down the stairs and Jonnae was hot on his heels, yelling and pointing her finger all at him.

"There's no reason why I should come home and have to park behind somebody else's car, another bitch at that," she screamed.

"YO!" I yelled. "I just fucking told you that she's here for me. If you had a problem, all you had to do was ask us to move the car. It's not that fucking serious." I instantly copped an attitude. She stopped and stared at me before rolling her eyes and walking off. I stared at her until she disappeared.

"What's good Alicia?" Capo said once Jonnae was gone. "Damn bruh, I see what you were talking about." Jaynell popped her head up off of her mother's shoulder.

"See. So the test wasn't even needed."

"Yeah, not at all," Capo agreed. There was an awkward silence that fell upon the room.

"Aye," I spoke up. "You mind if I leave my whip here while I ride with Alicia so we can talk?" I asked Capo.

"Nah, that's fine."

"I need you to move Nae's car though." Capo walked away and came back shortly after that with Jonnae's car keys in his hand.

"Actually," Alicia said. "Can we take your car? I'll explain why later." I could see a look of nervousness over her face.

"That's fine," I told her. It was as if just those simple words lifted a weight off of her shoulders. Within ten minutes, we were pulling away from Capo's house. I kept stealing glances at Jaynell through the rearview mirror. "So, tell me what's been going on."

She proceeded to tell me about how her life had been in Connecticut. She went on to tell me about the guy she was dating and how she ended up in the situation she was in.

"I lucked up when I dialed your number. I'm surprised you even have the same one after so long," she said. I shrugged but didn't say anything. "Listen, I know I was wrong for how I went about this whole thing with our daughter and I will apologize to you for the rest of my life."

"So let me ask you this , if you weren't in this situation, would you have ever told me that I had a daughter?"

She became quiet. I looked back and forth between her and the road waiting for her answer.

"I-I don't know."

"You don't think that I deserved to know that I have a daughter?"

"I'm sorry. I just didn't think at the time that it was the right thing to do. I need to know that you will take care of her."

I sucked my teeth. "Come on now. That goes without saying. I just hope she doesn't shut down because she doesn't know me."

"She does. Even though you didn't know about her, I made sure she knew who you were. I still have the picture we took when we were fifteen. It's hanging up on her wall in her room at my house. She always made sure to say good morning to the picture in the morning and good night to it at night."

"So what did you tell her if she ever asked about me?"

"I just told her that you didn't live in the same area as we did but that you loved her very much."

I didn't say anything. The car became extremely quiet.

"So what's going to happen to you once you go back to Connecticut?"

She shrugged. "Truthfully, I'm so tired of looking over my shoulder every time I go somewhere. I hate that I have to stay cooped in my house every second of the day but as long as I had Jaynell with me, I had to do what I had to do to stay safe. Now that she'll be with you, I'll accept the consequences, whatever that may be."

"Lee, are you ready to die?" I asked her seriously. I pulled over on the side of the road because I really needed her to look at me and tell me that she was ready to die. I saw the tears as they began to fall down her face.

"No, but I have no other choice. Monroe doesn't give a shit and it's my fault that it happened so I have to live with it," she sniffled and wiped her face as she kept her head down.

"Have you tried talking to them?"

"I don't know who 'them' is," she said looking at me. "Monroe won't accept any of my visits and he doesn't call me. I doubt he's even worried about the fact that I'm living how I am. I can't believe I even thought he loved me."

"Why don't you stay here?" I couldn't believe the things I was saying. Here I was dating Jass but wanting to protect Alicia. I didn't know if it was because she was my child's mother or if I still cared about her. Maybe it was a little bit of both.

"I can't. I'm not going to continue putting my daughter life in danger. It's okay Jarell. As long as my daughter isn't harmed, I'll deal with whatever happens."

I stared at her as she continued to play with her hands.

"Look at me," I told her as I cupped her chin and made her look me in my eyes. "Go back to Connecticut, get whatever little things have sentimental value to you and bring your ass back here. I'll keep Jaynell until you get back and I will get you set up here. I'll put you up way out in Newport if I have to but I can't just allow my daughter to continue to grow up and not have either parent with her. Do you understand me?"

She nodded her head. I pulled back onto the road and headed out to Oakland Beach. It was the end of summer, so I figured Jaynell would enjoy some time on the beach as Alicia and I played catch up, on shit that happened over the last four years.

Chapter Thirteen

Capo

I couldn't believe the resemblance between Alicia's daughter and Jarell. That shit was almost scary. The moment that they left, I went back in the house to find Jonnae. I had a few choice words for her ass with the way she came up in here earlier.

"Nae," I called when I walked back inside. She didn't answer so I went upstairs towards our bedroom. I walked in and found her sitting up with her back against the headboard. "What the fuck was that shit about?" I questioned her.

She rolled her eyes and kept looking at the television as if she didn't hear me. I stepped in front of it, preventing her from watching it.

"Why are you trying to talk now? You weren't trying to

say anything when your brother called himself checking me earlier," she retorted.

"Your ass came in here, blowing a fuse and I heard him tell you outside that she was here for him," I said moving towards her.

She rolled her eyes and continued to flip through the channels. I wanted to knock the attitude right out of her.

"Whatever. That still didn't give his ass a right to come and disrespect me in my house."

"Jonnae Myiesha Carter," I knew she could tell by my tone that I was dead ass serious. "If I felt for one bit that he was disrespecting you, I would have checked his ass and you know it. You just don't like the fact that somebody finally shut your ass up. Whenever you see a broad around me, you think it's something going on. I did that shit with Alani and it was a mistake. Now she's long gone so you have nothing to worry about. I've been telling your ass since we got back together that if I wanted to be with somebody else, I would be long gone. I'm where I want to be. Don't think because we have kids that I have to stay here with you because I don't."

"Yeah I know you keep saying it, which has me thinking that you really don't want to be here. Trust me, I'll never keep you where you don't want to be."

"Jonnae shut the fuck up because now you're starting to piss me off. Ja'kahri and Ja'kiyra do not keep me here. My love for you keeps me here but as of lately, you've been making it hard for me to not want to shove my foot in your ass," I told her honestly.

"I'm making it hard? You're not the one dealing with muthafuckers threatening you and shit."

I looked at her confused. "What the fuck are you talking about? Who threatened who?"

"Oh, now you care?"

"Jonnae don't make me slap you. Who threatened you?"

She smirked and went back to flipping through channels. I didn't know if she couldn't find something on TV or if she was just doing it just because.

"I will push this fucking TV off of the dresser if you do not answer my fucking question," I told her raising my voice and stepping towards the TV.

She sucked her teeth, "I went and saw Erick's mother."

"Even after I told you that you had no reason to go?"

"Obviously I did have a reason or else I wouldn't know that she thinks you had something to do with his death."

"How does she even know me?"

"I swear you don't listen to shit I say! I told you that they were close. He told her that you were the one who shot him in the knee a while back."

I couldn't believe that bitch ass nigga did all that shit popping and went running back to his mother like a little fucking punk.

"She had your name and everything so I'm guessing because he told her that Boog was there, that she put two and two together then figured you were my kids father. She told me she would hate for something to happen to my kids," she explained. At that moment, it felt like smoke was fuming from my ears. I didn't know who this lady thought she was but when you bring my kids into shit, you automatically signed your death wish. I was trying hard to keep my hands clean but it felt as if I was constantly being tested with some shit.

"Who is this lady?"

"Don't you think you have enough going on?" she asked.

"I'm not gonna ask you again. Give me her name and number." She sat there staring at me as if I had ten heads. "Whether you give it to me or not, I'll find out. You of all people should know about the connections I have."

Reluctantly, she grabbed her phone and scrolled down to her number. She slid it across the bed. I picked it up and looked at it. Pulling out my phone, I stored her number.

"What's her name?"

"Elaine Jackson."

"Why you acting like it's killing you to give up the information on the bitch who basically threatened your entire family? Why do you even give a fuck about any of those muthafuckers?"

"You're going through enough! You can try and hide shit from me but the streets talk Ja'kahri! I won't be surprised if the cops come knocking at my door again for your ass. I'll tell you what though," she stood up and turned off the TV. "If you keep bringing that street shit to my door, you won't have to worry about whether or not I feel like you want to be here. I'll leave with my kids. I'll be damned if I don't feel safe in my own fucking house." She stormed past me and I heard a door slam. I would deal with this attitude later. Right now, I had to find out where I could find this nigga's mother. One thing you never fuck with is my kids; that will have you pushing up dirt faster than you could blink.

Chapter Fourteen

Jonnae

Capo had me fucked up. He didn't think I knew about the shit he had going on but I wasn't the same young, dumb and naïve Jonnae that his ass met. Erick's mother wouldn't randomly mention his name if she didn't have a strong inkling that he had something to do with it.

I sat in the hallway bathroom until I heard the front door close. I peeked my head out first to make sure he really was gone. I then went to check on the twins who were both still sleeping. I went downstairs and found Janiylah passed out on the couch again. She had been shopping all morning with me in preparation for the twins' birthday.

I couldn't believe my babies were going to be one in less than two months. They both were almost standing up on their own without having to hold on to anything. Kiyra tried taking steps but she always fell after about three. Kahri didn't even try.

I went into the kitchen to get started on dinner. I was glad that everyone was sleeping and that Capo was gone because it allowed me to let my thoughts run free and figure a few things out in my mind. Once I pulled out everything to cook, I picked up my phone and called Michelle.

"Hello," she answered on the third ring.

"Hey, what are you up to ?"

"Nothing. I was thinking about going shopping."

"Come keep me company," I suggested.

"Your brother isn't there, is he?"

"No, I haven't seen him in a few days," I told her truthfully. "You haven't seen him?"

"No, I left the other day when he pulled that 'this is my house shit' and I haven't been back since. I only reach out to him when it's regarding the baby and that's it. Other than that, I have nothing else to say to him."

"Damn." I didn't know Michelle and Boog's problems were that bad. "Well come by, we'll sip on soda and pretend it's wine as we vent to each other. The kids are sleeping, Janiylah is passed out and I'm in dire need of some girl talk. Plus, I'm cooking."

"Girl you should have said that from the beginning. I'll be there in ten minutes." She hung up before I could say anything else. I couldn't help but laugh at her crazy ass. I cleaned the fat off of the chicken breasts and sliced them up. Tonight I would keep dinner simple with homemade chicken tenders and fresh French fries. I wasn't a fan of all the frozen, premade shit.

Just as I dropped the first batch of chicken and fries into the separate pots of grease, my doorbell rang. I figured it was Michelle. I grabbed the hand towel and went to let her in.

"Hey Mi-," I was stopped in my tracks by the boys in blue. My heart dropped into my stomach.

"Hello Ma'am. I'm Detective McDonald and this is my partner Detective Green. We are looking for a Mr. Ja'kahri Turner. Is he here?"

"No he's not. Can I help you?"

"Just let Mr. Turner know that it is in his best interest to contact us immediately." He handed me a card with his number on it. He turned and walked away. Just as they pulled out of my driveway, Michelle pulled in. I couldn't do shit but shake my head. I knew this shit was going to happen but Capo's ass swears he's fucking invincible. It's always something with his ass and he never fucking learns. But he was about to learn the hard way.

Chapter Fifteen

Boog

After waking up from my nap, I glanced around and noticed very limited light in the house. Through the curtains I could see the sun beginning to set. I checked my phone and noticed it was after seven at night. I didn't have a text or missed call from Michelle.

"Fuck it, two can play that game," I said to nobody in particular.

At that moment, my phone rang breaking the silence in the house. Without looking and automatically thinking it was Michelle, I answered.

"Yo, where you at?"

"Hello to you too."

I looked at the phone and realized it was Kitty on the other end.

"What the fuck do you want?" She was definitely the last person I wanted to talk to .

"Do you gotta be so ignorant?"

"Katherine," I said calling her by her government name, "after that shit you pulled, I don't even know why you're still dialing my number."

She sucked her teeth.

"It wasn't even that serious."

"What the fuck? You showed up at MY house and told MY girl that you're pregnant with MY seed. Fuck you mean, it ain't that serious? I told you off rip, I wasn't claiming shit until a DNA was done. I know I wasn't the only nigga that was hitting that. So how the fuck is you so sure that's my seed?"

"Jonathan, you know just like I know you've been the only one I've been fucking since you've been home."

I chuckled, "I've been home damn near two years and you tryna tell me that I'm the only person you've fucked in two years? We weren't even fucking on the regular so I know for a fact I wasn't the only one. There's no need to lie, if you were fucking somebody else then so be it, to each is own."

"I didn't call you for this," she said.

"I'm still tryna figure out why you called me, period."

"I want to at least be civil dammit."

"Do you know what civil is? Civil is what we were before you decided to do the shit you did. So ask yourself that question. Can you be civil?"

I knew she was getting pissed but oh fucking well. Nobody told her to be extra as fuck for no reason and pull the shit she did.

"Whatever, Jonathan," she replied, followed by hanging up .

I hated being hung up on but I didn't even trip. It was better that I didn't because the way I as feeling, it would have taken an army to stop me from driving to her house and breaking her face.

I dialed Michelle's number. I was starting to miss her. Lately we'd been going through it and I hated the strain in our relationship. After six rings, she hadn't answered. I hung up and redialed again. I got the same response. I tossed thoughts around in my head about where she could be. I started dialing her mother's house number but opted out. Instead I shot her a text.

Me: *where you at?*

I tossed the phone on the table before getting off the couch and heading to the bathroom. I flicked on both the living room and kitchen lights on the way. After using the bathroom, I checked the kitchen for something to eat. Before she left, Michelle had filled the cupboards and fridge with her snacks and cravings. I chuckled, as I moved her jar of dill pickles and grabbed my left over Chinese food. As it warmed up, I thought back on the last few weeks. Kitty had caused a lot of uproar recently and drove a wedge in the middle of our relationship. But I couldn't blame anybody but myself. I was fucking with Kitty before Michelle and once during our relationship. After our last time together, I told Kitty I couldn't fuck with her anymore. She took it easy, or so I thought. I never would have thought she would come back and cause this much drama.

The beeping from the microwave broke my thoughts. I grabbed my food and headed back into the living room. I sat and stared at the wall as I ate. So much shit was going on lately and I needed to gain control of it quick. Just as I finished, my doorbell rang. I dropped the container in the trash and the fork in the sink before I went to see who was on the other side. Looking out the window, I saw Capo's car parked on the street in front of my house.

"What's good, bruh?" I said as I opened the door and dapped him up. I stood to the side and let him in.

"Shit man. Nae just dropped another bombshell on a nigga when I was at the house."

"What happened?" I asked as I closed the door and followed him into the living room.

"She went and met with her ex's mother. Apparently when we gave the nigga a limp, he went back and told his mother my name. Now her ass is digging her nose in shit."

"Why would she randomly tell Nae that though?" I was confused.

"Because his ass told his mom that you were there too and she knows that you're Nae's brother."

I figured Nae must have told him about me when they were dating because I only remember meeting the nigga a handful of times. I know for a fact, I never met his mother.

I shook my head and sat on the couch.

"This shit is crazy. I already have this love triangle bullshit going on with Michelle and Kitty. Now I have to deal with this shit with this clown. He won't go away and the nigga is fucking dead," I said out loud. Before Capo could say anything, the vibration from his phone stopped him.

"Yeah," he answered. He was quiet as he listened to whoever was on the other end. I checked my phone to see if

Michelle had answered my text. "I didn't get any missed calls from you," he spoke again. I looked at him then at my phone. I was kind of disappointed that she hadn't. "Shit. A'ight, I'll be there shortly." He ended the call and looked at me.

"What happened?"

"Shit just went from bad to worse. The boys in blue are looking for me again," he told me.

"How you know?"

"Nae just said they came by the house." Capo sat down and looked like he had the weight of the world on his shoulders.

"Talk to me."

He sighed. "Your sister said some shit before I left the house that's weighing on my mind heavy."

"What she say?"

He sighed, "She told me that if shit kept getting brought to the crib, she's taking the kids and leaving."

"Come on now, you know Nae isn't going anywhere," I told him sounding more confident than I felt.

"Man I don't know. This is the second time in a few short months. She's been through so much."

"Capo, Nae loves you and the kids adore you. You think she would take them from you?"

"For their safety? Yes!"

I was left speechless. I could only hope my sister wouldn't but she was a mother before anything. Her motherly instincts would kick in first and she would anything to protect her kids. I couldn't blame her.

Chapter Sixteen

Michelle

"Nae, was that the cops?" I asked her as I walked inside the house and closed the door behind me.

"Yup."

I followed her into the kitchen and watched as she pulled her chicken out of the pan. My pregnant ass instantly got hungry even though I made a sandwich before I left my parent's house. But chicken was my favorite.

She picked up her phone and dialed a number. I listened as she told Capo that the cops had come to the house, looking for him again. It wasn't long before she hung up.

"What were they here for?"

She sighed as she dropped more chicken in the grease and pulled the fries out. I snuck a piece and tried to eat it but it was too hot.

"Busted, greedy," Nae joked. I smiled and put it down in front of me to cool off a little bit. "Capo got his ass into some more shit."

"Again?"

"Apparently. I told him if he keeps bringing this shit to my door, I'm taking my kids, his sister and I'm gone. Janiylah's about to start school, and she doesn't need this type of stress. She damn sure doesn't need to be in an environment where the cops are showing up every other damn minute."

I had to agree with her on that. Nobody wanted the cops at their door. every time they turned around.

"Have you heard about the shit with your brother and I?"

"What, that his old bitch showed up at the crib?"

"Yeah that, and the argument we had."

"I didn't hear about the argument."

I watched as she moved around the kitchen and thought about my relationship with her brother. If he had his shit together, I would have no problem making sure he came home to a hot meal; even if it was something as simple chicken and fries.

"I told him I wasn't feeling the fact that his ex bitch was coming to my house. He told me that she didn't come to my house, she went to his, so I left and I haven't been back since. That was a couple of days ago. I don't plan on going back any time soon. I need your brother to figure out if he wants to be with me or not. If not, I would rather know now and move on with my life."

"Damn," was all Jonnae said. "I know Boog loves you though."

"I know he loves me and I love him too but I love me more. I won't stand around and be anybody's fool."

"I completely understand. You have to do what you have to do. This is why I never wanted any of my friends to date his ass. I never want my relationship with my brother or my friends to change because of their own issues. You know what I'm saying?"

"Yeah, I feel you. Regardless, I would never make you choose between our friendship and your brother. That's why I haven't bothered you with our shit. You have your own family and drama to deal with. You don't need our bullshit to add to it."

She smiled at me and finished taking her food out. Just as she did, I heard one of the twin's start crying.

"I'll be back," she said as she turned off the stove and took off up the stairs. I looked at Jonnae's life then compared it to my own. I couldn't imagine going through the shit she was going through. I thought my situation with Jonathan was tough but it seemed as though she had it worse, plus she had two kids involved. My baby was still an fetus.

"Who's that?" I heard Nae say. I looked as she walked in the kitchen with one baby on each hip.

"Hi auntie's babies," I said.

I took Kahri from her hands and sat him on the counter in front of me. You would never known he was just asleep because he greeted me with his drool filled smile, showing off his two teeth. I kissed his fat cheeks as Nae strapped Kiyra into her high chair.

"Come on Kahri," she said as she grabbed him and strapped him into his. She then started shredding pieces of chicken and placing it on the tray in front of them.

"You seem like such a natural," I told her as I watched her move around.

"What do you mean?"

"At being a mom. It's like it just comes to you."

"It's not easy Chelle. Trust me. I had no choice but to learn. I didn't have my mother there to show me anything. I couldn't rely on anybody to help me because these are my kids. Only difference is, I had two so I had to do everything double. There were many sleepless nights. Capo helps me, but when he's not here, I'm alone. Janiylah is a big help and I don't even ask her to be. I would have probably lost my marbles a long time ago if Niylah hadn't been here these last few months."

I nodded.

"I'm scared," I admitted. Tears filled my eyes as I stared at her.

"Of what?"

"Failing."

"Michelle, there is no book on parenting. There is no guidelines you have to follow or anything. You do what you feel in your heart is right. As long as nothing you're doing is causing harm to you or your child, then do it. It'll come to you; trust me. It's an instinct that us women have. Everyone thinks because they see how loving Capo is with the kids, that I have it easy. I don't. This will be the second time this year that he has been involved with the law; so besides being a mother, I have to hold him down and help him through his problems. Truthfully though, my kids keeps me going. Being with a man of Capo's caliber isn't easy but my kids make me want to fight for it."

"How do you know when you've had enough?"

"When you know you've given your all and are receiving nothing in return. You'll know when you've had enough. If I leave Capo over this shit, I can tell you, it won't be for good. But if these cops and this jail shit becomes a constant reoccurring thing, then I'll be gone for good. I would do it all for the safety and stability of my kids."

I didn't say anything as I looked down at the table. My emotions were getting the best of me.

"You'll be fine, Michelle. I promise you'll be a great mother and regardless, I'll be here for my niece or nephew."

I looked up and smiled at her. I was glad that I had her by my side. I knew this journey wouldn't be easy, but I would walk it with my head held high and take on anything that was meant for me. It was time for me to start living for not only myself, but my child as well.

Chapter Seventeen

Alicia

I didn't want to argue with Jarell about me coming back so I just did what he said. I was scared shitless to go back to Connecticut and especially alone. I wouldn't be surprised if the only reason they hadn't come for me was because I had Jaynell. I was paranoid the entire ride back home. I did the same thing that I did on the way down. I constantly looked in the rearview mirror for anything suspicious. It had been three days since the last threatening call I had received. I knew it would only be a matter of time before I was contacted again and if they were watching me, I'm sure they would know I no longer had my daughter.

When I reached Connecticut, it was a little after five in the evening. My heart was racing. I was getting a bad feeling in my stomach and didn't even want to go to my house. I figured I would be in and out, in less than an hour.

I pulled up to my house and searched my surroundings. I couldn't help but to cry at what my life had become. I sniffled and wiped my face as I killed the engine and got out. I looked around as I walked up to the front door. I opened my house door and closed it quickly behind me, locking it. That was a big mistake.

"I've been waiting for you," a deep baritone voice spoke from behind me. I jumped and kept my back to the door. I couldn't help but to cry again because I knew I was not leaving my house alive. I wished I could have kissed my daughter again or even told Jarell that I still loved him.

"What do you want with me?" I asked with my voice quivering. I'm sure they could tell that I was beyond nervous. I was shaking badly and was only two seconds away from pissing on myself.

"Now don't act that way. You already know what this is about," he said as he continued sitting on my couch. The tears raced down my face and I didn't even try to stop them.

"Please," I begged. "If I have to work for a long time to pay you back, I will but please don't kill me. I have a daughter," I said.

"I know and if it were up to me, I would let you go but seeing as how I have a job to do, that's not possible. I hate to see a beautiful, young woman caught up in this type of nonsense. The problem is, your dear boyfriend, Monroe is pinning this all on you stating that you robbed him," he explained. I twisted my face and cried harder. *How could he* I thought to myself?

"No, I would never purposely do something like this and

put my daughter in harm's way. I hate that I even agreed to do it for him. Please," I begged and cried harder. I felt betrayed and wanted to crawl in a hole. I now knew why Monroe stopped trying to reach me. He had basically set me up to be killed when he told them I robbed him.

"I'm sorry little lady," he said as he raised his gun to me. I put my hands up and cried harder but my cries fell on deaf ears, as I felt the first hot bullet pierce my stomach. My hands went down to that area as another piece of hot lead hit my chest. My body fell to the ground and I was struggling to breathe. I laid face down when I heard the shooter walking over to me. He placed the barrel to my head as another tear slid down my face. I closed my eyes then asked God to protect Jarell and my daughter. I hope he would remind her how much I loved and cared about her. I wanted her to know how sorry I was for getting myself caught up in this situation.

"I really am sorry," he said as the final bullet ripped into my head, then everything became black and silent.

Chapter Eighteen

Jarell

It had been a week since Alicia had gone back to Connecticut. I was starting to get nervous because she never returned. I had been calling her phone and it went straight to voicemail. I called all types of hospitals and jails that were in the three-hour radius from Rhode Island to Connecticut. Nobody had any information on Alicia. I couldn't lie; I was beginning to fear the worse. I remembered where Alicia's mother had lived years ago and only hoped that she still lived there.

Capo agreed to watch Jaynell for me. I hoped she didn't give him a hard time. I had been spending a lot of time with Capo, Janiylah and the twins so that she could get used to them. At night, she stayed at Capo's. I had yet to tell Jass about her. There were so many times I wanted to but I didn't know how.

I pulled up to Alicia's mother's house on the East Side, damn near on Blackstone Blvd. I had always admired where Alicia grew up. You could always tell this was where the doctors and lawyers in town lived. Last I recalled, Alicia's mother was a doctor but was going back to school to become a brain surgeon.

I walked up to the front door and rang the bell. I looked around and noticed the two cars sitting in the driveway. The navy blue Audi A8 and the cocaine white C-class Benz were both clean.

"Can I help you?" a voice asked me. I turned around and came face-to-face with Alicia's mother, Dr. Linda Jenkins. Her face hadn't aged at all from when I was seventeen until now.

"Hi, Ms. Jenkins. You probably don't remember me, but I'm -."

"I remember you," she cut me off. "You're the same boy that got my daughter pregnant. What the hell do you want?"

"Look ma'am. I'm not here to hear you bash me on something I knew nothing about. If I didn't think something was wrong, I wouldn't be here."

"What are you talking about?" she asked as she crossed her arms across her chest.

"Alicia called me last week. She came down and told me that she got herself into some trouble with somebody down in the city she was living in. She asked me to take care of her daughter, who I'm just finding out is my daughter. I told her to go back and grab anything of value then come back here. I was putting her and our daughter up in a house.

That was a week ago. I've been calling her phone. At first it was ringing a few times and then going to voicemail but now it's just going straight to voicemail. I've called hospitals and jails all within a three-hour radius of here and Connecticut. They all said there is nobody at the jails with that name or in the hospital that matches her description. I think she's in trouble," I explained. By the time I was done talking, Alicia's mother was holding her hands over her mouth.

"I-I'll call her father. I haven't talked to her in years. Anything I know about her or my grandchild was told to me by her father. Please, come in." She stepped to the side and let me in. She wiped her face just as she picked up her phone. I admired her living room as she called Alicia's father.

"Allen, it's me. When's the last time you spoke to Alicia?"

I looked at her as she waited for him to answer.

"Can you stop by her house and check? I have her daughter's father here at my house. He said he's been calling her for a week and can't get in touch with her."

She got quiet again.

"He has their daughter," she said.

I rolled my eyes. All of these questions could have been answered later.

"Call me as soon as you get there."

She ended the call and turned her attention towards me.

"He's gonna go by there and call me." I nodded and the room became quiet.

"Where's Jaynell?"

"She's with my brother," I answered.

"Do you think I can meet her?"

I nodded again. I know Alicia hadn't spoken to her mother but I would never not let her see her granddaughter. She smiled and hugged me.

"Thank you." Before I could respond, her phone rang. "Hello."

I held my breath as I watched the color drain from her face. I knew it couldn't be good news.

"Oh God, No," she screamed as she dropped to the floor. There was nothing else that needed to be said. I couldn't stop the tears as they welled in my eyes and slowly began cascading down my face. I bent down and hugged Ms. Linda tightly. I noticed her phone was on the floor. The call to Alicia's dad was still connected. I picked it up and put the phone to my ear.

"Hello?"

"Hello," a male voice answered. I could hear the shakiness in his voice and my heart dropped again.

"My name is Jarell. I'm Jaynell's father. W-what happened?" I stuttered.

"Uh, um, I-I just found Alicia in her apartment dead. Her body has already started to decompose so I'm sure she's been here for a few days. I'm waiting for the cops and ambulance to get here now."

I closed my eyes and pressed my lips together as the tears fell again.

"C-can you see any visible wounds?"

"There was a lot of blood around her head and I'm guessing it was a shot to her head. Once they get here, I'm sure they can give me more answers."

I nodded as if he could see me as I still held Ms. Linda

tight. She was still crying.

"I have to call my wife and let her know what's going on. Can I have your number to call you directly once I find out anything new?"

I shot off my number for him and we ended the call. I held onto Alicia's mother.

"My baby! Why? What did she do?" I wished I had the answers for her but I didn't want to tell her what Alicia had said because I didn't know if it was truly them or not. "I have to get to Connecticut," she said.

"I can't let you drive in this condition. You won't make it," I told her honestly.

"Can you go with me?"

I was torn. Here just twenty-minutes ago, this lady was ready to judge me based off of some shit that happened four years ago and now she needed me more than ever.

"Can you give me an hour? I have to handle some things first and I will gladly take you there." She nodded and stood up before wrapping her arms around her body. I plugged my number in her phone and handed it to her. "If you need anything before then, do not hesitate to call me."

She nodded her head again and sat on the, couch rocking back and forth. I took another look at her before heading out. I called Jass and told her to meet me at Capo's right now. I then hung up and dialed my brother's number. I told him that Jass was on her way and that I planned on telling her about my daughter. Although I loved Jass, if she couldn't accept my daughter then she would have to keep it moving. Now more than ever, my daughter needed me.

Chapter Nineteen

Capo

I could hear it in Jarell's voice that something wasn't right. I hoped it wasn't anything with Alicia although, deep down inside I was almost certain that it was. I looked down at Jaynell playing with her dolls that her father bought her. She had warmed up to all of us rather well plus she always had fun with Niylah and the twins.

"Nae?" I called.

"Yeah."

"Can you do me a favor?"

She nodded as she pulled Ja'kiyra out of the high chair and laid her on the couch to change her diaper.

"I think something happened to her mother," I said pointing to Jaynell. "Rell said Jass is on her way here and he's gonna tell her about his daughter. I don't really want the twins, Niylah or Jaynell around for that matter. I know how Jass can get. You think you can take them out for about an hour or so?"

"I got you."

I smiled. Reasons like this, I was glad for the mature side of Jonnae. Sometimes she had her moments when she was childish but when I needed her to be an adult, she always was. She finished changing Kiyra then changed Kahri.

"Janiylah," she yelled. Niylah came flying down the stairs so fast that I thought she fell. "Want to go do some more party shopping?" Niylah smiled and didn't say anything as she took off back up the stairs.

"I'm guessing that means yes?"

"She's a girl. When isn't she down for shopping?" I couldn't help but laugh. I knew then that Janiylah hung around Nae too much because she was back downstairs in two minutes flat.

"The kids coming too?" she asked.

"Yeah. I'm not sure if Rell left her booster seat but I check by the front door," I told her. Luckily he had. *Smart move Rell* I thought to myself. Within ten minutes flat, the five of them were out of the house. It was perfect timing because Jasmine and Jarell were pulling up at the same time. Rell pulled in first and was out the car before Jass had her car fully parked.

"She in there?" he asked me. I shook my head no. I didn't know who he was referring to but it didn't matter since nobody was here besides me. Rell waited outside as Jass got out of the car. I left the door open as I went and grabbed me a beer out of the fridge. Although it was still early afternoon, I was sure after this conversation, I might need something harder. Jass wasn't about to take this news lightly but I was going to be here to make sure that nothing went flying.

"Why did you ask me to meet you here?" she asked the moment they walked inside. Rell closed the door behind her and I sat at the barstool facing the living room.

"I have to talk to you about something very important."

"Okay. What is it?"

He sighed. "First and foremost, I want you to know that I lo-."

"Yeah, yeah. You love me. I know that. What the hell do you have to tell me?" Jass asked, cutting him off.

I couldn't help but chuckle. Jass was a feisty one and she didn't try to hide it at all.

"I found out last week that I have a daughter." My eyes bucked because I was surprised that he came right out and said it. I thought he was going to stall a little bit.

"You what?" she popped up off the couch like a Jack-In-The-Box. "You cheated on me you stupid motherfucka?"

"No I didn't cheat on you, Jasmine. She's almost three. I knew nothing about her up until last week when her mother called me."

"So you want me to believe that some random bitch called you, said you have a daughter and you just believed her?"

I watched as Rell cringed when Jass called Alicia a bitch. I knew how much Rell loved Alicia at one point. I wouldn't be surprised if he still did love her.

"If you sit the fuck down and listen, I can explain it."

"Oh, I'm listening but I'm not sitting down." She

crossed her arms across her chest. "Talk."

"Before I met you, I was with this girl, Alicia for almost three years. Out of nowhere, she up and moved without so much as a word. I now know it's because she found out she was pregnant and her mother made her go to Connecticut to live with her father. I don't know what led to her telling me after all of these years, but she did."

"Have you even seen this little girl? How do you know she's yours?'

"She's been here for the past week. She's been staying here with my brother."

Jass cut her eyes at me. I threw my hands up in defense. My loyalty lies within my brother. He asked me not to say anything, so I didn't.

"So everyone is around this bitch playing happy go lucky family while Jass is walking around looking like a dumb bitch? Y'all Turner's are something the fuck else!" she shouted. Her antics weren't fazing me one bit so she could keep yelling if she wanted to.

"Where is her mother?"

Rell dropped his head.

"I found out today that she was killed when she went back to Connecticut." I choked on my beer. I knew I didn't hear him right.

"You serious, bruh?" I spoke up for the first time. "What happened?"

"I would rather not speak on it until I know all the facts. I just came from her mother's house and she just found out. She wants me to take her to Connecticut to find out what happened."

"Wait a minute! You think I'm supposed to be okay

with you going with your ex bitch mother, up to another state?"

"Jasmine! Enough with the bitch comments," Rell snapped. "I would never allow anybody to disrespect you and I would appreciate if you would do the same to the mother of my child."

"Oh, so I'm supposed to accept this with open arms?" she questioned

"Quite frankly, whether or not you accept it, my daughter isn't going anywhere. You can stay and deal with it or get to stepping, the choice is yours. If you're leaving, I expect you to be gone by midnight tonight. My daughter will be moving in first thing tomorrow." I sat in shock as I watched the whole situation go down. Rell was never one to come at anybody, especially a female without a reason but Jass was asking for it.

"You know what. I'm out. You can have your happy little fucking family. I'll be gone before you know it." She got up and left as Rell sat on the couch, looking as if he had the weight of the world on his shoulders. The moment I heard the front door close, well slam, I walked over to my brother.

"You good?"

"I'll be fine. Do you mind keeping baby girl tonight? I wanna find out what happened with Alicia and at least grab anything I think will be valuable for Jaynell."

"That goes without saying. She's been enjoying the twins as well as Niy and Nae. She'll be good. Go handle your business bruh."

Rell stood and dapped me up.

"Good looks. I owe you bruh."

"You would do the same for me."

He smiled and jogged out the door. If I didn't feel as though my family was being tested before, I knew for sure we were being tested now. But we were going to overcome this test like we overcame so many others.

Chapter Twenty

Jonnae

After an hour and a half of buying outfits and decorations, the kids had crashed while me and Janiylah were starving. We packed everything into the trunk, packed the kids into the back and headed to the house.

"You ready for your junior year, Niy?" I asked her.

"I think so. I won't lie though, I'm kind of nervous."

"Why?"

"Because after this, it's senior year and then off to college. It feels like it all went by so fast."

I smiled. "Don't worry about it. You'll be fine. I must say though, I'm very proud of you. Despite all that you have been through, you have grown into an amazing young lady. I can't thank you enough for all of the help that you give me with the kids."

"Thank you. If I didn't have my brothers behind me, I wouldn't know what to do."

"Trust me, they are proud of you too."

The rest of the ride to the house was quiet. My mind wandered a little bit. I glanced in the rearview at Rell's little girl. It was scary how much she looked like him. Parenting wasn't easy but since Capo and Rell both played a major part in raising Janiylah, I'm sure Rell would do a great job. I could only help but wonder how Jasmine would react to it though. She wasn't the easiest person to share news with.

Twenty minutes later, we pulled up to the house. I called Capo to ask him to come outside and give us a hand. Once we got everything in the house, I laid the kids in their cribs and laid Jaynell in Janiylah's bed.

"Man, I'm glad you took the kids," Capo said as I reached the last step. He was sitting in the living room with his feet kicked up on the table. Janiylah was in the kitchen, making something to eat.

"Why, what happened?"

"Well Rell told Jass about Jaynell and Alicia then she flipped out."

"I'm not surprised. What did she say?"

"Basically Rell told her either she accepts Jaynell or she can leave. If she's leaving, she needed to be gone by midnight because he's moving Jaynell in tomorrow." Capo seemed to find humor in it.

"What she say about that?"

"She told him, she wasn't accepting it and she'll be out. But check this, Rell had to rush to Connecticut because they found Alicia dead in her house."

My hands shot over my mouth. We may have had a bad introduction but I never wanted her dead. I couldn't imagine my babies living without me. My prayers definitely went out to Jarell and especially their baby girl.

"Damn. That's sad."

"I told him we would keep her tonight."

I nodded but didn't say anything.

"So what's gonna happen as far as you calling the detectives?"

"I called my lawyer and he contacted them. They said they just want to ask me some questions so we're going up there first thing Monday morning."

I swallowed hard. The last time Capo walked into the police station, he didn't come out for over a month.

"Are you sure they just want to talk?"

"They have no evidence. But speaking of that, I have to make a call. I'll be back." He stood and walked away. I followed him with my eyes and couldn't help but wonder what other shit he was about to get himself into.

I got up and went into the kitchen. I made myself a bologna and cheese sandwich then grabbed some chips off of the fridge. I sat at the table and became lost in my thoughts. I wondered about my mother. I hadn't spoken to her in about a month. Last I heard, she was in rehab again and didn't want anybody to contact her until she felt as though she was fully recovered. Capo paid the bill and vowed to pay it as long as she was there. I couldn't thank him enough for doing that. He and Boog still ran the streets, but with caution.

Capo had mentioned that he met this guy who owned a fairly new club downtown called Encore. I hadn't gone but

Capo went a few weeks ago and said it was nice. He was interested in doing something legal and making money. I knew this street shit couldn't and wouldn't last forever.

"What you thinking about?" Capo said almost scaring me.

"Nothing really."

"Come watch TV with me."

I finished off the last bite of my sandwich and cleaned up my mess. A part of me wanted to pry into Capo's business but the other part just wanted to sit back and trust my man. I decided that I would go with the latter . But if for one second I felt as though I couldn't, I wouldn't have a problem protecting what's mine at any costs.

Chapter Twenty One

Boog

Michelle and I were finally talking but it wasn't anything spectacular. I mean we had minimal conversation and it was mostly about the baby. If I brought up anything about our relationship, she would change the subject. My house was so fucking empty and the silence was starting to drive me crazy. I needed to bust a nut bad but Michelle was being stingy with the pussy too. A nigga couldn't win for shit.

I sighed and grabbed my keys before heading out the door. Just as I was about to start up my car, a cop car came from out of nowhere, blocking me in.

"Shit," I said under my breath.

"Step out of the car with your hands up," the officer said through his blow horn. I shook my head and stepped out of the car. I raised my hands and kicked the door shut. The cop ran up behind me and roughly placed his cuffs on.

"Why am I being arrested?" I questioned.

"Shut up, you piece of shit." He began to Mirandize me and led me to his car. From that moment on, I kept quiet. I had a bad feeling that it would take one hell of a fight for me to get out of this shit.

When we reached the Providence Police Department, it took them over two hours before they let me make a phone call. I thought about calling Michelle but she wouldn't do anything but ask questions and right now, I didn't need that. Instead, I dialed Capo's number. I knew once he heard the recorded voice, he would know what to do.

"Yo," he said once he accepted the charges.

"Shit looks bad bro. Call the lawyer for me and I got you covered," I told him.

"Done."

"Aye," I said before he could hang up. "Keep this on the hush." I didn't want Nae to know because she seemed to do irrational shit when she was pissed and panicking.

"Yup." We ended the call and I was led back to the holding cell. They tried asking me questions and I continuously refused to answer. They caught my attention though when they mentioned Kitty's name. It made me wonder what she had to do with this. I wasn't going to ask them shit because they would think that I would be willing cooperate with them.

I laid back on the hard ass bench and put my hands behind my head. I would rather do time again than to bump my gums to the boys.

"Carter," an officer yelled. I sat up and looked at the

bars. "Let's go." I walked over to the bars and put my arms through them as they cuffed me. They led me down a hall to a room where lawyers sat with their clients. Walking inside, I was blown away at the beautiful lady that stood on the side of the table. Even though she had on heels, she looked to be about five foot eight. She had cocoa colored skin and her hair was bone straight. I could tell she either just got a fresh perm or her hairstylist was a beast with the a blow dryer. I chuckled to myself at my thoughts. She looked to be a solid size fourteen but I wasn't complaining. I had to talk to myself to send a message down to my dick for him to stay down because he was itching to try and stand at attention.

"Hello, Mr. Carter. I'm LaToya Brown, your attorney." I heard the door close behind me and I figured the cop left. "Have a seat."

I sat down and she sat on the opposite side.

"Do you know why you're here?" she asked me.

"Not a clue. I wasn't tryna hear shit them niggas was saying because whatever story they're tryna concoct, I have nothing to do with."

"How would you know?"

"Because I don't chill with anybody and I mind my business."

"Well I'm going to call the officers in. I will do all of the talking. I want to find out what they think that they have you on."

"A'ight, sounds good with me."

She stood and walked over to the door before knocking on it. She took a few steps back before it opened and the arresting officer walked in with another guy in tow. I rolled my eyes at his ass.

"Mr. Carter, are you ready to talk?"

"How the fuck can I talk to you about something and I don't even know why I'm here?" I snapped back. My attorney grabbed my shoulder to calm me down.

"Officer…" she paused waiting for him to give her, his last name.

"McDonald. Detective McDonald."

"Oh, excuse me, Detective. Do you mind telling my client why he is here?"

"Well, for more than one reason. One, we know he was involved in a shooting alongside a Ja'kahri Turner."

My heart dropped but I kept a straight face.

"Also, we have a Katherine Conners claiming that Mr. Carter physically abused her," he finished. My face twisted up, I never touched Kitty. I haven't touched her ass since the last time we fucked. I shook my head as I thought back to Capo going through this same shit with Lani's ole trifling ass. I couldn't believe these bitches were that damn hell bent on making our lives hell.

"Do you have anything to say, Mr. Carter?" the detective asked.

"Nah, I'm enforcing my right to remain silent. I'll fight both of these bitches in court before I say anything to y'all muthafuckers."

"Very well. The choice is yours," the detective stood up and pushed his chair in. "You're not new to our system so the judge will not be easy on you."

"Let me tell you something," I said leaning forward. "Last time, I was young and dumb. I fell for the bullshit and accepted whatever punishment was given to me without fighting it. I refuse go through that shit again. So I will fight until I can't fight anymore."

I sat back and kicked my feet up on table.

"I believe if you do not have anything to hold my client on, then he is free to go," Ms. Brown said as she stood up. I stood up too and starting walking to the door.

"Actually," the detective said. "We have a relative of the victim that states she was told you were there."

"Now detective, you know just like I know that in this line of business we can not go by hearsay. We need solid evidence before we have a case. When you have that, contact my office and not my client." She tossed her business card on the table and followed me out of the door. The moment that we stepped outside of the precinct, she turned and looked at me.

"I'm not saying they don't have a case, but as of right now, they don't have a strong case. I will continue to work on this and try to see what they have going on but I need you to stay clear of either victim. Well, the one victim," she corrected.

"That's the thing, I haven't even touched the 'victim' in months and that's physically, sexually or whatever way you want to consider it," I told her.

"Then they have to prove that you did. I'm thinking that will be an open and shut case. As far as the shooting, we have to see what they have before we can do anything. I'll be in contact with you and Mr. Turner soon."

"A'ight. Thanks again."

She smiled and turned to walk away. I couldn't help but stare at her ass. A car honking broke me from my trance. I looked to the left and saw Capo laughing then shaking his head at me. I chuckled and walked over to his car.

"You just don't learn nigga, do you?" he asked as I closed the door behind me.

"A nigga can look."

"Looking will get your ass hurt too. Anyway, what they saying?"

"Supposedly Kitty saying I abused her and they talking about some shooting with you."

He released a hard breath and shook his head as he drove away from the station.

"I'm guessing it's the shit with this nigga Erick's mom . She has to be talking about when he was shot in the knee because she is just reaching on the murder shit. But he ain't here to testify and what he told her wouldn't be considered a dying declaration. This nigga Chauncey was supposed to be taking this rap for this shit since his ass didn't clean the fucking scene like he was supposed to. I told that nigga he had forty-eight hours and that was two weeks ago. He just signed his own fucking death wish ."

I listened to what Capo said and shook my head. It blew my mind how a nigga could accept a payment for some shit his ass never did. It was cool though, because like Capo said, he had just signed his death wish.

Chapter Twenty Two

Michelle

I dialed Jonathan's number for the fiftieth time and it went straight to voicemail. The damn police station wouldn't tell me shit and I was a nervous wreck. I didn't know if I should call Jonnae and ask her because I didn't know if she knew anything but I was out of options. When I came to Jonathan's house, his car was in the driveway but his neighbor told me that the cops arrested him before he could leave.

Just as I was about to connect the call to Jonnae, I heard the front door open.

"Babe?" I called out.

"Yeah." I jumped off of the couch and went running towards him. Before he could think twice, I jumped into his arms and started crying.

"Shhh, why are you crying?" he asked me. I tried to answer but I couldn't. He rubbed my back and slowly started walking. He sat on the couch and I was still straddling his lap. After a few minutes, I got myself together. "Are you going to tell me what had you crying like that?"

I wiped my face and tried to climb off of his lap but he held me in place. I took a deep breath before I started talking.

"I came by here to talk to you about everything that's been going on. When I got here, I was about to unlock the door, when your neighbor told me that you had been arrested when you were trying to get in your car to leave. I thanked him, came inside and started calling your phone then the police station. The officer who answered the phone wouldn't tell me anything. I literally have been pacing this floor for hours. I kept contemplating on whether or not to call Jonnae but I didn't know if she knew anything or not. I didn't want to alarm her if she didn't."

"Relax, Ma. Yeah they did arrest me but they have nothing but a bunch of hearsay. My lawyer is working on it. Capo picked me up because he was the first person I called because I knew he would be able to get shit handled with little to no questions," he said. I twisted my face at him.

"Oh so you don't trust me?"

"It's not that I don't trust you. I trust you with my life. I just know you. You would have wanted me to explain everything to you right then and there. It wasn't the time or place for me to do so. I needed help and Capo had the access to what I needed at that moment. Trust me, it wasn't nothing like that."

I didn't say anything as I stared in his face. At that moment, I realized how much I loved Jonathan. I wanted our relationship and our family to work. I softened my face and wrapped my arms around his neck. I planted a soft kiss on his lips, followed by another and another.

"I've missed you like hell, Ma. We gotta get this shit right. I can't take you not being here and the silence in this house is driving me up a wall."

"I have a question."

"Ma, if it's gonna kill the mood, don't ask it," he said.

"But I have to know."

He sighed. "A'ight, what?"

"Is there a chance that you can be the father of her child?"

He looked at me deep in my eyes.

"Michelle, listen to me. I'm about to tell you the truth and after this I don't want to hear shit about this situation. Understand?"

I swallowed hard and my heart started beating faster. I nodded and waited for him to drop the bomb on me.

"When I first came home from my bid, I ran into Kitty. I fucked with her a little bit before I got locked up. When I got out, I went back to what I was used to. We had nothing more going on than fucking. It was just sex. When I met you, I'll admit, I fucked with Kitty from time to time because it was her that I was used to. I cut her off and she didn't take it to well. We fucked once like five or six months ago. She then called me with that bullshit that she was pregnant. I told her off rip that I wasn't the father because I never fucked her without a condom. I fucked with her for a long time, I can admit that but I know for a fact, I wasn't the only nigga that she was fucking. So no, that is not my child. I can say that with confidence and mean it."

I looked deep in his eyes and searched for any sign that he was lying but couldn't find anything. I softened my face and cracked a smile.

"I believe you," I told him and I meant it. I knew without trust, we had nothing. Yes, I was still upset about the bitch coming to the house claiming her child was his. But if my man said the child wasn't his, then I was taking his word on it.

Chapter Twenty Three

Jarell

I was in Connecticut damn near all night. By the time we got there, Alicia's crib was cleared of her body and any police. They had dusted her house for any suspicious prints and such. I met her father and extended my condolences. He thanked me for taking in his granddaughter and for going to Alicia's mother's house. Had she not called, he wouldn't have thought about going over to her house. He usually heard from Alicia about once a week. From the look of his eyes, I could tell he had been crying non-stop. Throughout the ride up here, I had to fight back my tears as her mother sobbed in my passenger's seat.

After speaking to Alicia's father for over a half hour, he let me into Alicia's apartment. I held my nose because the stench of a decomposing body was still evident. I couldn't help but lock eyes on the bloodstain that was on the floor. I caught a chill as I stared at it. It broke my heart, picturing Alicia lying and dying in her own pool of blood. I shook my head and headed in the direction of the bedrooms. The first room on the left I opened the door to was Alicia's room. I flicked on the light and smiled at how everything was in place. Even when we were younger, she was such a neat freak.

I looked at the shelves she had built behind the bedroom door. She was a picture junky. I was surprised to see some of the pictures we had taken together years ago. I noticed a few pictures with her hugged up with another guy and suspected it was the guy, Monroe that she said was locked up. I took out my phone and snapped a picture of it, so I would remember what he looked like. I planned on trying to find out as much as I could about this cat. The fact that he left her out here, high and dry had me feeling some type of way.

I looked around her room to find anything that I thought would be Jaynell's. I spotted a few stuffed animals but couldn't tell if they were Alicia's or Jaynell's. I turned and walked back to the kitchen to try and find a couple of garbage bags. I found a box under the sink. I grabbed it and hurried to her room. I had to move quickly because the smell was causing my stomach to turn. I grabbed any pictures of her and myself and put them in one bag. I looked through the drawers for anything important. When I reached her nightstand, I found her journal as well as a couple pieces of jewelry. I tossed it all in a garbage bag and made a mental note to go through the journal later on.

After fifteen minutes, I left Alicia's room and went into

Jaynell's. I flicked on the light and smiled at the Minnie Mouse theme she had going on. I made another mental note so I could have her room at my house decorated. I instantly locked eyes on the poster size picture of Alicia and I that hung on Jaynell's wall. I smiled because it brought me back to the day. It was short lived as my stomach began bubbling. I pulled the picture off of the wall and leaned it against the wall. I was glad that it was framed.

I tossed all of her clothes and shoes into a bag. I must say, Alicia did the damn thing with taking care of her. When I reached the closet, I noticed a lot of stuff still had tags on it and looked big. I smiled and sent a silent thank you to Alicia. I tossed everything into the trash bag and went through the small dresser that was on the side of her toddler bed. I found some jewelry that I assumed was Jaynell's by the size of it.

After spending almost forty minutes in the house, I was done. When I walked back by the blood spot, my eyes watered. I blinked them away and walked out of the front door. Her mother and father were still standing outside talking. I loaded everything in my car and ran back inside for the picture I had left in Jaynell's room.

"I'll start tomorrow on the arrangements and everything," her mother said as she wiped her face. My heart went out to both of her parent's; especially her mother because she hadn't spoken to her daughter in a while and never would get the chance to again. "I'm going to get a hotel room up here until after the funeral and everything. Do you want to stay too?" she asked me.

"Nah, I have to get back because I want to get Jaynell all situated and moved into my house. She's been staying at my brother's because he has kids as well as my little sister. By all means though, please let me know when all the arrangements have been made so I can come back up here," I told them. They assured me they would and I jogged back over to my car. I used the GPS to find how to get to the nearest gas station so I could fill up as well as grab a red bull. It would help me stay awake as I headed back to Rhode Island.

Within twenty minutes, I was on 95N back home. I couldn't believe that in the matter of a week, I had found out that I was a father and was now forced to raise my daughter without her mother. I shook my head. I really wished I had some adult female guidance when it came to this parenting thing. I would try to do all I can to the best of my ability when it came to raising my daughter.

It was after two in the morning when I reached my house. To say I was tired would be putting it lightly. The red bull was wearing off and I knew it was only a matter of time before I crashed. I thought about leaving everything in my car but the last thing I needed was one of the knuckleheads in my neighborhood to try in break into my car. I grabbed the bags and the picture then carried it all inside, making one trip. I left everything in the living room and locked the door behind me. I striped out of my clothes, said a silent prayer and allowed sleep to overcome my body .

Chapter Twenty Four

Capo

I was up early, making the three little ones something to eat. I knew with everything that had been going on lately, that Jonnae was tired. So when the twins woke up this morning, I quickly climbed out of bed before she could wake up. After I grabbed them and put them in their highchairs, then I went back to Janiylah's room and saw Jaynell sitting up in bed while Niylah was still sleeping. I smiled at her and grabbed her out of the bed.

I sat her at the kitchen table and turned on the small TV we had in the kitchen and put on cartoons. The three of them easily became engrossed while I made them scrambled eggs and a few sausage links for Jaynell. Once everything was cooled off, I put the eggs in front of the twins and placed a small plate in front of Jaynell. I poured a plastic cup full of juice and fixed a bottle to go with the twin's eggs. Once they were all set and eating, I went back in the kitchen and fixed me a bowl of cereal. As I sat at the table, I thought about everything that was going on. I thought back to Boog calling me yesterday telling me he was locked up. When he told me why they had arrested him, my mind began racing.

The last thing I needed was another fucking case on me. Seeing as how the shit with Lani hadn't been over for a good couple of months, I didn't want to get involved in that shit again. I made a mental note to call LaToya again so she could tell me what we were looking at. I know I had to go tomorrow to speak to these stupid fucks so I wanted to know what I was up against.

I finished my food and cleaned up the mess that the kids had made. They were sitting still watching The Fairly Odd Parents as I cleaned up the kitchen. Just as I finished, the doorbell rang. I wanted to cuss out whoever was on the other end because I knew Nae would wake up after that. I dried my hands off and went to open the door. I calmed down when I found out it was Rell. He looked like he was ready to fly off the handle.

"I'm gonna kill that bitch, bruh," he said as he rushed passed me and instantly starting pacing the floor.

"Whoa, calm down. What happened?" I asked as I closed the door behind him. I hadn't seen Rell this hype in a long time.

"Bruh, so I got back late last night from CT and shit. Once I got to the crib, I put everything inside and went to bed. I wake up this morning, my nigga she tore everything the fuck up in my crib, besides my damn bed!"

"What? Who Jass?"

"Who else? I mean she sliced my couches, broke every damn dish and cup in the kitchen, the bitch even pulled my clothes out of the closet. She cut some and bleached the rest. I'm ready to take that bitch head clean the fuck off of her shoulders. As if I'm not going through enough, I gotta deal with this shit too?"

He finally stopped pacing, sat on the couch and put his head in his hands. I felt bad for my brother and I wished there was something I could do to help him but I had my own shit going on.

"Have you tried calling her?"

"Hell nah. It wouldn't make me want to do shit but find her and beat her ass."

"We don't need you to do that shit. You've never been the type to put your hands on a female so don't start that shit now."

"I know, which is why I had to come over here and talk to you first. I swear, you would think I cheated on her or some shit."

"Females react different to things. Although I knew for a fact that Vanessa's son wasn't mine, I know had that test came back that he was, Nae would have left me."

"But you and Nae have kids together so that's different. Me and Jass don't have shit but a relationship."

"You're missing the point," I told him. "If a chick is getting into a relationship with you and you have no children, they want to be the first and only one in your life. They don't want to hear about a blast from the past and some maybe babies."

I looked at Jarell as he sat in thought.

"I just thought she would be here forever. Ya know?" I could tell my brother felt defeated.

"Listen to me, Rell. If it's meant to be, then Jass will be back. If not, then fuck it. You have a beautiful two-year-old baby girl in there. You'll be sent someone who will be there for you and be a wonderful mother, well stepmother to Jaynell. For now, just be a great father to your daughter because she needs you now more then ever."

"Thanks, bruh. I appreciate you and Nae for all y'all have been doing for me this last week," Rell said.

"Jarell, as long as I am alive, I'll always be here for both you and Niylah."

I gave my brother a hug and walked off as my phone rang. I was expecting a call from that nigga Chauncey's baby's mother. The money hungry bitch was willing to turn his ass over for a punk ass thirty grand.

"Yo," I answered.

"I just talked to him. He said he'll be here in twenty-minutes to see the kids."

"A'ight." She lived in Chad Brown so it wouldn't take me but all of fifteen minutes to get there.

"Hey," she called before I could hang up. "Thirty racks right?"

"Yeah. I told you, you'll get ten up front and twenty when his ass is convicted."

When I first reached out to her, she wasted no time spilling the tea and going on and on about how much she couldn't stand him. She was tired of his empty promises to their kids. He would come by and use her for sex, visit the kids for an hour then leaves . He also used her as his own personal punching bag sometimes.

She could do whatever she wanted to do with the money, the nigga was going to to pay for accepting my money and not doing a job. I don't tolerate that shit. I ran upstairs to find Nae sitting in bed.

"Aye, Ma. I gotta run out for a few. The kids are downstairs watching cartoons and Rell is down there with them. I don't know how long he's going to be here. I'll be back as soon as I'm done."

"Okay," she replied. She puckered her lips for me to kiss her and I did. I gave her several pecks before rushing out. I knew I had to beat this nigga there because I planned on being inside the house when he came in. He fucked with the wrong one.

Luckily, the highway wasn't crowded so I was able to speed and get there in no time. I was glad there were no cops around because the last thing I needed was to attract one of those bitches. I parked my car on the street and called to let her know I was outside. I looked around before jogging over to where her apartment was.

"He should be pulling up any minute. The kids are sleep but I didn't tell him that," she rushed and said as I followed her into her apartment. "Do you have the money?"

I cut my eyes at her.

"Is he here yet?" She shook her head no. "Then no, I don't have the money. Come on now, if you think I'm the type of person to do some shit like this and not pay then baby girl you better ask about me. Shit, my money is the reason why this is even happening."

I didn't want to say too much to this chick because I would hate for her to catch a case of loose lips and her children are forced to become orphans.

Before she could answer, we both could hear a loud beat system coming down the street. I noticed she rolled her eyes.

"That's probably him. For whatever reason, he always has to make a damn scene when he rolls up somewhere."

He better enjoy these scenes while he can I thought to myself. I sat on the couch then thought about it and stood up.

"What door is he coming in?" I asked her.

"The front."

I stood out of the way, behind the front door and waited for his ass to come in. It wasn't long before he killed his loud ass engine. I now knew why he blasted music; his car sounded almost a thousand times worse than it looked.

"Yo, Dee," he yelled as he opened the door. He pushed the door closed and I pushed the gun to his lower back.

"You thought you could run forever bitch, but I always find who I'm looking for," I said in his ear as I felt his body tense up. He knew he had fucked up and there was nothing he could do about it.

Chapter Twenty Five

Jonnae

I heard Capo's conversation with Rell and it had me feeling some type of way. I loved Jass and I fucked with her the long way but to do some hood rat shit like that when the nigga didn't do a damn thing to you was fucked up. That called for an ass whooping but knowing Rell, he wouldn't even take it that far. Me on the other hand though, I would have no problem tagging her ass. I don't take to kindly to people fucking with family.

When I heard them wrap up their conversation, I tiptoed back into the bedroom and climbed in bed as if I had never left it. It took everything in me to not call Jass the moment I got to the room but I knew my eavesdropping would blow up in my face. For now, I wouldn't say shit.

Once Capo left, I headed downstairs to talk to Rell

myself. He looked as if he had the weight of the world on his shoulders. I took Jaynell down from the chair, she was sitting in and placed her on the floor in front of her father. I took the twins out of their high chairs and sat them next to Jaynell. They were all engrossed in the cartoon that was on, which was good because I would be able to have a decent conversation with Rell.

"You a'ight?" I asked him.

He sighed and rubbed his hands across his face.

"I will be. I just never imagined shit turning out like this. Plus, this shit with Alicia is fucking up my head."

My heart went out to him because I couldn't imagine not only finding out you just had a child but also then your child's mother gets killed.

"I'm sorry about that Rell and for going off the way that I did when I met her," I told him sincerely.

"Plus I wake up this morning to find my house in fucking shambles. I didn't notice it yesterday when I got home because I was so damn tired but when I woke up, I was ready to slap this bitch," he said getting visibly pissed.

"What happened?"

He went on to tell me what happened with Jasmine the day that they had the conversation when he told her about Jaynell then what he woke up to at his house.

"Are you sure it was her?" I asked.

He looked at me sideways.

"She is the only one who has a key to my house and there was no damn break in. Plus, it was some shit only a bitch would do. I know she only did it because I told her I was moving Jaynell in today. Now I have to wait because my house is completely fucked up besides my bed."

I shook my head. Jass was petty for that shit.

"You know all you have to do is say the word and I'll be on that ass," I reminded him seriously. He laughed and shook his head.

"Capo would never let me put you in that situation."

"I'm sure he would rather me beat her ass than for you to go to jail behind beating her ass. Like I said, say the word and she's mine."

"Nah, it's a'ight sis. Thank you though," he said chuckling. I hugged him and sat back.

"Are you hungry? I see Capo fed the kids but did he offer you something?"

"They must've ate before I came because they've been watching TV since I been here. But I'm good sis. I'm about to go clean up my house and go get my baby girl a bedroom set. I can take her if you want," he said.

"Jarell don't be dumb. It's fine if she stays here. I gotta give it to Alicia though, most children her age are hyper or all over the place but she's so calm and quiet, I forget that she's here. She plays well with the twins and everything."

He smiled as he looked at his daughter. I could see the love he had for her in his eyes.

"Before I met her, I was upset that I missed out on everything. I thought that we would have a strained relationship but when I laid my eyes on her, all my anger melted. I instantly fell in love with her and I'm beyond grateful that Alicia told her who I was, so she wasn't afraid when she met me. I'm glad she warmed up easily to you guys too. I just wish Alicia was still here and we both were able to watch her grow into an amazing lady."

"Alicia will always be with you and her. The same way

Alicia told her about you, make sure you tell her about Alicia and how much she loved her. I will be here to help you in any way because being a parent is not easy but it's very joyful."

"Thanks, Nae and like I told Capo, I owe y'all so much for all that y'all have done for both Jaynell and I over the last week. I appreciate it more then you will ever know."

"Don't even worry about it. It's what family does," I assured him. I patted his knee and got up to head to the kitchen. I knew Niylah would be up soon and she would probably be hungry and ready to rummage through the kitchen.

"Nae, how's your mom?" Rell asked me. I froze in my place and dropped my head. I was missing my mom and hoped that this would be her final time in rehab.

"She's doing okay, I guess. I haven't seen her lately. She's back in rehab and doesn't want anybody to see her until she knows for a fact that she is clean."

"Oh okay," was all he said. I took a deep breath and continued into the kitchen. I whipped up a quick omelet that I was sure Janiylah would eat. Just as I finished, she came into the kitchen rubbing her eyes.

"I hope you made enough for me," she said as she sat at the island.

"Yes greedy," I laughed as I slid her plate in front of her. "Rell do you want some?" I called out.

"What is it?"

"Food, nigga," I joked. I could hear him laugh. "Nah, it's an omelet."

"Yeah I'll take some." I cut a piece off of Janiylah's on her plate and she gave me the death glare. I laughed and cut a piece off of mine and made up Rell's plate. I gave him his plate and sat at the island with Niylah to eat.

"Do you know how many classes you have this year?" I asked her. I knew she would be starting school within the next week and still needed clothes as well as school supplies.

"Yeah, my schedule came in the mail the other day."

"Alright, once we get the kids dressed, we can go shopping for clothes and supplies."

"Okay."

I looked at Niylah as she ate and couldn't help but smile. I knew it must be hard losing your mother and never knowing your father but Janiylah was growing up to be an amazing, young lady. I could only hope that her mother was proud of the young lady that she was becoming and happy that I was in her life and doing all that I could for her. I know I could never replace her mother and I wouldn't try but if I could be a positive role model to her then I would be.

I made a mental note to talk to Capo about enrolling the twins into daycare. I know he would throw a bitch fit at first but I don't know how he expected me to continue on with my education, if I was always home with the kids. He ran the streets too much to be home with them so he would have to get over himself.

Chapter Twenty Six

Boog

I hadn't realized I dozed off on the couch with Michelle until my ringing phone awakened me. I slowly eased my hand out, careful not to wake Michelle to reach my phone on the table. I noticed it was Capo.

"Yo," I said in a raspy voice. I cleared my throat a little and shifted.

"Yo," he said loudly. I turned the volume down some.

"What's up?"

"Can you talk?"

I looked down at Michelle, who looked to be sleeping peacefully. I hated to move her but I wanted to have this conversation in private.

"Hold on." I put the phone back down and lifted her off of me. I laid her back down directly on the couch, grabbed the phone and headed outside. The sun was setting, which gave off a nice sunset on the horizon. "A'ight, what's good?"

"I caught that nigga slipping at his baby mama crib."

"Who?"

"That nigga Chauncey. I'm about to slide through real quick to fill you in. I'm only around the corner."

"A'ight." I hung up the phone and waited for Capo to pull up. I went down to my car to check and see if I had a pre-rolled blunt in there. Luckily, I did. I pulled it out and sparked it just as Capo pulled up. We both jumped into my car, I cracked the window and I passed the blunt to him.

"As I was saying," he continued as he inhaled the smoke. "I caught him at his baby mama's. He thought he was going to continue to run but you know a money hungry bitch will do pretty much anything for a quick buck. I forced that nigga to admit that he did it and I drove his ass to the station myself."

"Damn, that easy?"

"Nah, not that easy. That shit cost me another thirty racks. The nigga won't tell me what he did with the other fifty I dropped off to him. It is what it is though. I have a nice amount of money left over and I want to go legit. I got to go holla at this nigga downtown, who owns that new club. He is supposed to put me up on going legit and shit. I don't know if I want to own a club though."

"Whatever you choose, you know I want in on it. I can't do this street shit forever."

"You already know. I was sitting outside this nigga baby mama crib when I called you. I dropped his ass off at the station then had to go back to her crib to drop off the ten grand."

"A'ight. Is LB is going to be calling us soon?" I asked. I needed this case to be over. I had a little one on the way that I needed to be straight for.

"Probably. I've had her on payroll for a while so I'll go holla at her. I'll keep you updated on this shit though."

"A'ight. If you need anything, hit my line."

"I got you."

We ended our conversation, he dapped me up and climbed out the car. I got out and sat on the porch for a little while longer. I stared off at the sunset and let my mind run. When I got out of jail, I never imagined shit going like this. I mean, I knew I would jump back in the streets to get some money up but I never imagined being wrapped up in some bullshit. I needed LaToya to figure out this shit with Kitty's ass too. I made a mental note to holla at LaToya tomorrow about that case. If Capo said he had the murder shit handled, then I could focus on this shit with Kitty and get that straightened out so I can go on with my life.

I heard the door creak open behind me. I turned around to see Michelle standing there rubbing her eyes.

"What are you doing out here?" she asked.

"I was talking to Capo and I didn't want to wake you so I came out here. You okay?"

"Yeah."

I looked down at her growing baby bump. Michelle was now eighteen weeks pregnant and was finally starting to show. We found out next week what she was having. I knew she couldn't wait because she was itching to start planning the baby shower. It was all she talked about after we discussed me being arrested.

"Are you hungry?" I asked her.

"Yeah, I'm about to whip up some spaghetti real quick. You want that or something else?"

"That's fine. You have everything in there or you need to go to the store?"

"No, everything is here. I have the hamburger in the sink thawing out under some running water. If you want to go get garlic bread and something to drink you can," she suggested.

"A'ight, bring me my keys and my wallet."

She turned and disappeared but came back shortly after with both. I gave her a kiss and walked down the few steps that made up our porch. Just as I reached the bottom, my phone rang.

"Yo," I said noticing it was my nigga Knuck.

"Aye, you around?"

"I'm leaving the crib, why?"

"Swing through real quick. I need to holla at you."

"A'ight." I knew swinging to see him would detour me from the store but it was straight. I knew if he was calling, it was either about some shit he felt like I needed to know or some money. Both were important. I found a half smoked Black & Mild in the ashtray and lit it up. I cracked the window and took off to Parkis Ave. where I was sure Knuck was. Ten minutes later, I pulled up and like clockwork, Knuck jogged over to my car.

"What's good nigga?" I greeted as he climbed inside.

"Shit man. Now you know I hardly ever call you to the block…"

"Unless you got some important shit to tell you or if it's about some money," I said cutting him off. I knew my nigga like the back of my hand.

"Exactly. Well it's both. You know I'm always out here, even if I'm not hustling. Apparently, one of these niggas been fucking with some chick you know because she was bragging to him about how she was about to set you up to do some time," he said. My blood was boiling and he hadn't even said who it was. I was positive it was Kitty's bitch ass though.

"Who?"

"Let me get there. This nigga, Justin been fucking with some chick Katie or Katherine or some shit like that. Anyway, I'm guessing they was pillow talking and she said some shit about how if you wouldn't take care of her kid then you wouldn't be taking care of your bitch's kid either. Justin said he got pissed because he was laid up with the bitch and she talking about another nigga but he said he just listened. She went on and on about how she called to speak to some detective. Justin said before she went on some more, he told her that he heard enough and left. I don't know if he knows that I know you or not but this nigga was just going in on her. You know who it is?"

"Yeah that's Kitty's bitch ass."

"Oh shit, I didn't even know that's who he was talking about."

"They arrested me yesterday on some shit with her but my lawyer is looking into it. I swear these bitches out here be tryna fuck a nigga all the way up."

"Well you know I had to put you up on that. The other shit though, the connect I have is bullshitting like a muthafucka. I don't have time to be trying to wait for him to show his face. There is too much money to be made to be playing those games. I know you gotta know somebody?"

I had my boys who pushed my work for me on a couple blocks and made me good money. But if I could get Knuck on my side, I could probably double it and leave him to this shit when I finally decided to call it quits.

"What you need?"

"A couple bricks. What's the price?"

I thought about whether or not I should tell him that I probably had what he was looking for. Fuck it. He had been my nigga since we ran these streets as teenagers.

"I got them for eighteen."

"Word?" he said as his eyes bugged. "I was paying twenty-one."

"How many you want?"

"Let me get three for now."

"A'ight. Can you give me a few hours? Two tops?"

"Yeah that's fine. I got enough to hold me over until tomorrow or Friday but I'll need to reup by then."

"A'ight. You'll definitely have it by then," I assured him.

"A'ight."

We chopped it up until I made it back around to Parkis Ave. I dapped him up and told him I would be hitting him up shortly. We parted ways and I headed off to the store to get what Michelle wanted. I was sure she was going to bitch about how long I had been gone but she would be a'ight. Business called first.

Chapter Twenty Seven

Michelle

I was draining the pasta when Jonathan walked back through the door. I figured he made a couple of stops in between because it didn't take an hour to go to the market and back.

"My bad, Ma. I had to run and see my nigga real quick but here," he said as he slid the gallon of pink lemonade and the bag of garlic bread on the counter. I didn't say anything as I poured it back into the pot and buttered it. I turned on the oven for the bread and continued what I was doing.

"Go wash your hands, the food will be done in a second unless you want to wait for the bread to be done."

"Nah it's fine." He walked towards the bathroom as I poured the sauce over the pasta. I was learning to let

Jonathan be a man and not smother him by asking his constant doings and whereabouts. Sometimes it was hard, but I was getting there. I was at least grateful that he returned home every night, unharmed. He came back with a hand towel drying his hands as I was making our plates. I double-checked on the bread in the oven, grabbed the Parmesan cheese and we both sat down. We made small talk as we ate. I missed times like this and cherished when we had these moments.

I took the bread out of the oven and sat back down. Once we finished, I cleaned up and washed dishes as Jonathan said he had to run back out. I wanted to ask him where he was going but I refrained. He said he would be back and I believed him. I finished doing the dishes and cleaned the kitchen. I popped a bag of popcorn, put in an old Disney movie and climbed on the couch. I decided to watch the movie *Mulan*.

Almost two hours later, Jonathan still hadn't returned. My nerves were getting the best of me. I shot him a text message and changed the movie since it was over. I grabbed a couple more snacks and sat back down. I tried to focus on the movie but I kept glancing at my phone, hoping that a text message or phone call would come through. I looked at the time and it was well after ten. I picked up the phone and dialed his number but I got the voicemail. I left him a message telling him to call me as soon as possible.

It was almost midnight, when he came walking through the door. A part of me wanted to go off but the other part was happy that he was home.

"I'm sorry, Ma. I got caught up chopping it up with the guys and lost track of time. By the time I went to call you, my phone had died."

"It's cool," I told him. We were finally getting back on the right track and I didn't want to go back to the constant arguing. He kicked off his shoes and came and sat next to me on the couch. He tried snuggling up under me but I wasn't trying to have him touch me.

"Come on, Chelle. I told you I was sorry." That was it; I couldn't hold it back anymore.

"Sorry? Sorry? Let me go out and come home four hours later with no type of call or text and just tell you that I'm sorry. Sorry doesn't fix shit Jonathan. I've been sitting here worried sick and you just stroll the fuck in like everything is good. Yes, I'm glad that you're home safe but a courtesy call or fucking text would have been great."

"I can't go back and redo the shit. I said I'm sorry and your ass still isn't satisfied."

"You know what, I won't say shit else. Stay out all damn night if you want to but when I start doing it, I don't want to hear shit." I got up and headed to the bedroom. He could stay his ass out there for all that I cared. If he wasn't worried about how I felt, then I wouldn't worry either.

I laid down and placed my hand on my stomach. The fluttering feeling I felt made me smile. I couldn't wait until I felt the actual kicking. I especially couldn't wait to find out what I was having. I had an idea for a boy baby shower but I didn't want to start planning until I knew for sure.

It wasn't long before I felt relaxed and started dozing off. I welcomed sleep with open arms.

Chapter Twenty Eight

Jarell
Four Days Later…

Today was the day that I had to make the trip to Connecticut with Jaynell to lay Alicia to rest. She had been asking for her mother lately and although I knew she didn't understand much, I told her that she was with God. I hated to even bring her but both of Alicia's parents begged me to. I strapped her into her car seat and went around to hop in the driver's side.

"You ready?" I asked her as she looked at me. She smiled and nodded her head. I was impressed by Jaynell's intelligence. For an almost three-year-old she was advanced. She could spell her first name and count to twenty. I was glad that she was adjusting well to life with me. I planned on enrolling her in a daycare that I thought would fit her and meet her intelligence level.

I played music softly and headed for the highway. I figured Jaynell would end up falling asleep on the ride. My mind wandered to Jasmine. I couldn't lie; I was missing her like hell. I wished she would have made this situation easier and stuck around but it was what it was, I guess. My main focus now would be my daughter.

Three and a half hours later, I pulled up outside of the funeral home. The parking lot was damn near full. I looked around before I killed the engine. I looked back at Jaynell, who was fast asleep in her seat. I shook my head as I got out and walked around to get her out. She lazily opened her eyes as I lifted her out and put her head on my shoulder. I locked my door and headed inside of the funeral home. I knew I was late so a few people that were there would probably look at me.

I walked in and was greeted by one of the funeral home workers. I shook his hand and walked inside, where the rest of the small funeral guests gathered. I spotted Alicia's parents sitting on the left of the casket. Her mother had tears racing down her face and her father was trying to comfort her. There was another woman who sat in the front row and wore a death glare on her face. She was cutting her eyes hard at Alicia's parents. I'm guessing it was Alicia's stepmother.

Alicia's mother spotted me first and waved me over to her. As I walked by, I couldn't help but look at Alicia's body lying in the casket. She looked beautiful in death just as she did alive. I felt a lump forming in my throat. I really couldn't believe my baby girl was gone.

"Thanks for coming," her father Allen said to me as he shook my hand. I smiled as I handed him a sleeping

Jaynell. He hugged her tightly and kissed her. Linda then reached out to take her from him and held her. She cried harder as she snuggled her face into her neck. Jaynell began waking up and looked at Linda. It was sad that she never met her granddaughter and it was even worse that it was under these circumstances but now that she was with me, they would have a relationship.

I pulled Alicia's father to the side as Linda sat back down with Jaynell on her lap.

"Have you heard anything else?" I asked him as we walked outside.

"No, they have no type of leads on anything. It just really hurts me because my daughter didn't deserve this," he said as he started crying again. I toyed with telling them what Alicia told me. I knew her parents deserved closure.

"Mr. Collins," I spoke up. "When Alicia came down to see me, I asked her what made her reach out to me after all of these years. Ya know, I knew nothing about Jaynell up until she called me. She told me that she had got caught up with some people behind her ex boyfriend Monroe. She said she had been receiving threatening phone calls about some money that was stolen from her."

Right in front of me, her father looked as if the color in his face was draining from it.

"You okay?" I asked him.

"I told her that Monroe was a bad guy. I knew he was bad news and now my daughter is gone."

Watching her father break down did something to me. I hated that her family had to go through this.

"Son, I just want to thank you for stepping up and being there for my granddaughter. If it's the last thing I do, I will get justice for my daughter, one way or another. Truthfully, I'll be satisfied if Monroe never sees the light of day again at all. It would be better if he was dead though."

I nodded as I listened to him.

"If you need anything sir, let me know. I know you don't know me but I'll help in any way that I can. I loved Alicia and although it's unfortunate that she's gone, I'm grateful to have a piece of her left here. I promise to take care of Jaynell to the best of my ability," I told him honestly.

"Just keep her in our lives. She is all we have left of our only child."

"I will Mr. Collins. I have one question though," I said as he wiped his face to try and stop the tears from falling.

"What's that?"

"Who is the lady that was giving both you and Ms,. Linda the death glare that was sitting in the front row?"

"That was my wife, Patrice. Even though Linda and I haven't been together in over fifteen years, she can't stand the fact that Linda was the only one to give me a child. Almost a year after Alicia was born, I got into an accident at work and crushed my testicles, causing me to never be able to have children again. I've always looked at Alicia as my blessing. Although Patrice loves me, she's always wanted children. I told her that we could adopt and she refused. She said if she couldn't bear them, then she didn't want them. She loved Alicia and was by her side when she came to live with us, but she always had a dislike for Linda.

"She has been giving me the cold shoulder for the last week of Linda being here. She knows why she is in Connecticut but she feels like we still have something going on. I have told her over and over again that Linda and I are nothing more than two parents grieving the loss of their child. If she gave me any shit during one of the hardest days of my life, I would have divorce papers drawn up so fast, her ass wouldn't even blink. So she has just been sitting there with a pouty face. As long as she don't say shit, we're good," he said. I couldn't help but laugh because he was so serious.

"So why did she even come if she was going to sit there with the pissy faced?" I asked.

"Because she loved Alicia."

I nodded in understanding.

"Come on," he said. "Let's go back inside. We're doing everything today because we're going to cremate her. I will be sure that you and Jaynell get ashes."

"Thank you."

Together we walked back into the funeral home. We got there just in time because Ms. Linda was calling him up to the podium as she held Jaynell on her hip.

"Um, before we end," she started. "Allen and I would like to say a few words and maybe Jarell, Alicia's daughter's father would like to speak a few words as well."

I was shocked because I wasn't prepared to say anything. My mind started racing as I thought about what to say.

"When I gave birth to Alicia, I felt a sense of happiness come over me. I was twenty-five and fresh out of med-school. I was afraid that I wouldn't complete it because I was pregnant but she gave me a push of motivation and determination to want to push on for her. The day she was born, I knew what my purpose here was. It was to give my daughter the best life she could have asked for and give her a positive female role model to look up to. When she was sixteen, she came to me and told me she was pregnant," she said as she paused and looked over at Jaynell and kissed her forehead. "My only regret in life was giving my daughter the ultimatum of having an abortion or leaving my house. She chose to leave and live with her father and for that, I not only missed out on my daughter's pregnancy when she needed me most, but I missed out on the birth and the first three years of my grandbaby's life.

"That is something that I have to live with for the rest of my life. I can't hold my daughter's hand through her contractions or help her get through labor. I can't kiss my daughter and tell her how much I love her and only wanted the best for her. I can't have girl talks with my daughter anymore, or shopping dates or anything of that nature; all because I was hurt at the fact that my daughter was pregnant and going to be a teen mom. If I could go back, I would have helped my daughter. I would have done anything I could to prepare her for motherhood. Although my heart is crushed that my baby girl is gone, I am so grateful for the fact that a piece of her was left here on earth for us to remember her with." She turned and looked at Alicia laying in her casket. "Alicia Brittany Collins, I love you and I miss you so much. Mommy is sorry for everything and I hope that you have forgiven me." She began crying as she walked back to the chair she was sitting in and placed Jaynell on her lap. I leaned against the wall as Mr. Allen walked up to the microphone.

"First, I want to thank those of you that came to show my daughter love on this sad day. I didn't realize how many people Alicia impacted in the three years of living in Connecticut." He cleared his throat and looked back at Alicia. "From the day I laid eyes on Alicia, I always called her my miracle baby. I didn't know why, but I did. About a year after she was born, I got into an accident at work, which hindered me from having any more children. It was then that I realized why I called her, my miracle. Alicia was the only child that I was blessed with.

"When I found out Alicia was going to be a mother at sixteen, I was crushed but when she stood her ground about keeping her child, I backed her up because I knew she would need parental guidance. Her mother had done an amazing job in the fourteen years of raising her alone. I was there financially but work kept me away often. When Alicia came to live with me and my wife Patrice, we showered her with parental love but also gave her tough love and reminded her that having a child wouldn't be easy. Boy, did my child prove that she was going to be something. She graduated high school on time and from day one, took care of her daughter. It was very, very rare that she asked myself or Patrice for any type of help. She moved out shortly after and had been taking care of herself ever since. I couldn't be more proud of my daughter. She knew if she needed anything, one call and daddy would be right there." A few people in the funeral home let out a slight chuckle. "Man, I'm going to miss my baby girl. I'm going to miss our conversations or her random house visits she did. Like her mother said, although this day is the toughest day of my life, I am thankful that we are left with a piece of Alicia here on earth. Daddy loves you baby girl; always and forever." He walked away from the podium and headed over to Alicia's casket to kiss her.

I guess this is it I thought to myself as I walked up.

"I wasn't prepared for this, so I ask everyone to bare with me," I said. "I'm Jarell, Alicia's daughter, Jaynell's father. I met Alicia when I was thirteen and she was twelve. We went to the same middle school together. I always found her pretty but back then, girls hung with girls and boys hung with boys. I kept an eye on her though because I knew one day, she would be my girlfriend. I ended up catching Alicia at the playground one afternoon and we spoke. After that day, we became best friends and she was actually my first girlfriend. She was the first girl that I ever loved besides my mother and sister. When my mother died when I was sixteen, Alicia helped me get through that tough time. I couldn't have been more thankful for her because I didn't know if I was coming or going. We dated for two years before she fell off the face of the earth.

"It wasn't until two weeks ago, that I found out why she left and that I found out I had a beautiful baby girl. Two days later, I met my daughter and fell in love with her. I made a vow that I will be in my daughter's life from that moment on up until my last day. I didn't think the day after meeting my daughter, she would lose her mother. Although my daughter is almost a spitting image of me, she reminds me of Alicia as well. It wasn't until I saw Alicia again that I remembered how much I loved her and still do. I hate that it had to end this way for her, but I'm so glad that I'll have my daughter here to remind me of her. Alicia," I said looking at her casket as if she was going to answer me. "I loved you then, I love you still, I always have and I always will. Rest peacefully, beautiful. Jaynell and I will miss you tremendously." I walked over and planted a kiss on her cold forehead.

I knew that Alicia's mother was bonding with Jaynell but right now, I needed to hold my daughter. I wanted to cry but I knew I had to hold it together; at least until I got back to my house. I grabbed my daughter from her grandmother and stepped outside. I hugged her tight and held her in the air.

"Daddy. loves you princess. It's you and I against the world, forever."

Chapter Twenty Nine

Capo

After I left the police station, I called LaToya and told her to check in with the detectives. They should have a confession by now. I knew that Chauncey's baby mama was counting on it because that would be the only way she got the other twenty racks. As I pulled off, I thought back on the entire encounter.

Once he felt the gun in his lower back, he tensed up. I pushed it deeper into his back, causing him to walk forward.

"Cap, man I can explain," he started.

"Explain what? You had over a fucking month to turn yourself in and you didn't. So what the fuck can you explain?"

His baby mama turned and walked away, leaving the

two of us to deal with each other. Well, more so for me to deal with him. I pulled the gun away from his back and walked around to stand in front of him, keeping the gun trained on him.

"I was going to," he said not sounding convincing at all.

"But what happened?"

"I wanted to spend time with my kids."

I laughed as I kept the gun pointed at his head.

"According to your baby mama, you come to spend maybe an hour with them and that's it. That leaves you twenty-three hours to do something and turning yourself in wasn't one of them. So in order to make sure that you do turn yourself in, I'm bringing your fucking ass to the station myself. I'm walking you in and I want to hear you tell them you're turning yourself in for murder."

He stood quietly and looked as if he wanted to cry.

"Would you make sure my kids are straight since I can't make a living to support them?"

"Where's the fifty grand your ass was paid?"

"Most of it is gone."

"Gone? What the fuck did you spend fifty grand on that fucking fast?"

"I-."

"Forget it. I don't even want to know. I got your kids though and that's my word." His baby mama would get the twenty grand after he was in custody and I would send her another two grand a month for the kids . If the kids weren't taken care of with that money, then that would something he has to take up with his baby mother.

"Can I at least kiss my kids goodbye?"

"Sure."

I followed him as he walked to his their room. I didn't want his ass to try and get any bright ideas like jumping out of windows or some shit so I stood at the door of his kid's room. His baby mama, Dee was sitting on her bed with the door wide open, staring at me. Her face was emotionless as she watched. I glanced back in the room as Chauncey was kissing his sleeping daughter's cheek. I started feeling bad but all of this could have been avoided. All he had to do was tell me he didn't do the job and returned my money or he could have completed the job like he was paid to do.

"Let's go," I said as he walked in front of me. I placed the gun on his back and followed him outside. He climbed in the passenger's seat as I climbed in the driver's side and pointed the gun at him.

"Man, you can put the gun down? I'm not going anywhere."

I looked at him sideways but put the gun down. I kept it on my lap with my hand wrapped around the trigger, just in case he decided to jump crazy. The ride to the station was silent. I had nothing else to say to him and it seemed as though he felt the same way towards me, which was fine.

I arrived at the station and drove into the garage, before tucking the gun under seat and out of sight. Together, we got out and headed inside.

"What am I saying again?" he asked.

"Tell them you're looking for the detective in charge of the murder on Miller Ave. They may ask you why, just tell them you're turning yourself in." He looked straight ahead and nodded. I walked inside the station with him and made sure not to make eye contact with any officer. I didn't need *them to try and pull me in.*

Within ninety minutes, I was gone and Chauncey was booked. Dee had been texting my phone nonstop asking what happened. She received a call from Chauncey, saying that he was being transferred and booked. I dropped the other twenty racks off to her and drove off.

I was glad this shit was over and done with. I just hoped Chauncey wouldn't bitch up in the end but for now, I could focus on my family.

Chapter Thirty

Jass

Six Weeks Later…

It has been almost two months since I had last spoken to Jarell and I was missing him something terrible. I contemplated calling him several times but I know after tearing his house apart the way that I had; I was probably the last person he wanted to hear from. I felt bad about what I did but I was hurting. At the time, it made sense but looking back at it, I regretted it more and more. I hadn't spoken to anybody that was affiliated with him. I thought about reaching out to Nae but I knew that she was going to lay in my ass for destroying his house.

It hurt me that Jarell had a child. I wanted to be the only one to bear his children. I looked down at my small belly and ran my hand over it. Three weeks after I left Jarell, I found out that I was twelve weeks pregnant. I wanted to tell him but I didn't know how. I knew he was going through a lot with his daughter's mother death and I just assumed he wouldn't be happy about this announcement. Nobody knew that I was pregnant. I found a job a month after leaving Jarell, at a beauty salon. I loved doing hair ever since I was eleven years old. I was so good at it that I was hired without having a license. Currently they had me doing braids on their male clientele and a couple of designs on kids.

I looked at the time and saw it was a little after eight at night. For the seventh night in a row, I toyed with calling Jarell to tell him about the baby and apologize for everything I had done including leaving him during a tough time. I sighed and slowly dialed his number. I put the phone to my ear as my heart beat rapidly in my chest .

"Hello," he answered sounding winded.

"Hi," I replied, just above a whisper.

"What's good?"

"How are you?"

"I'm doing alright. Jaynell don't touch that," he yelled. My heart crushed a little bit. A small part of me was still hurt by the fact that he had another child but I was learning to deal with it. "Sorry about that. What's up?"

"Um, do you think we could talk?"

"About what?"

"Us."

"Jass, we ended when you destroyed my house. But if you want to talk, you know where I'm at."

He hung up the phone before I could say anything else. I looked at the phone sideways before I put it down on the coffee table.

"Mom, I'll be back," I shouted as I stood up from the couch, slid my feet into my slippers, grabbed my keys and headed out the door. My mind raced as I drove in the direction of the house I used to share with Rell. I thought about what I would say to him and how the conversation would go. I wondered how he would feel about me being pregnant.

Fifteen minutes later, I pulled up in front of Rell's house and saw him sitting outside watching his daughter run around. I couldn't lie, the view made me smile. I took a few deep breaths before stepping out of the car. I got out, locked the door and walked over to meet Rell on the porch.

"Jaynell be careful," he called out. I took a good look at the little girl, who was running around chasing a butterfly, she thought she could to catch. I giggled. She was beautiful and she looked exactly like Jarell. It made me wonder what my baby would look like.

I walked over and sat on the step below him .

"What's up, Jass?" he said, without taking his eyes off of the little girl. I couldn't help but watch her too. At first, I didn't know what to say. I thought I had it all planned out before I got here, but all the words I wanted to say were no longer in my mind.

"You just going to sit there ?" he asked.

"I want to apologize."

"For?"

"Everything! For leaving when you needed me and for what I did to your house. It was uncalled for. If I didn't want to stay, I should have been woman enough to pack my stuff and leave without being petty."

"That's real big of you Jass. Real shit, I wanted to take

your head off when I noticed that shit, but instead I went and talked to my brother and Nae. After a long conversation they told me to cool off and think before I did anything I would regret. I took their advice and just decided to go home to clean up."

"I really am sorry Rell."

"Move your arms, Jass."

Without thinking about it, I lifted my arms that were covering my slightly growing belly. Once I realized what I was doing, I put my arms back down quickly, trying to hide it.

"How far along are you and when were you going to tell me?" he questioned. I didn't want to look at him because I didn't know if he was mad or not.

"A little over a month ago, I found out and I planned on telling you. I toyed with it since I find out but I didn't know, how you would feel."

"Do you see her?" he asked, pointing to his daughter running around. I nodded. "Her mother waited until she was in grave danger before she told me that she even existed. I never want to experience that shit again," he snapped. "I don't care what we are going through, when it has to do with my child, I want to know. You hear me?"

I nodded my head, quickly. I felt even worse as I watched the little girl trip and fall before getting back up to start chasing the butterfly again.

"I'm sorry and I don't want to be without you Jarell. I'm willing to accept your daughter as my own. I know I can never replace her mother but I want to help you raise her in any way that I can. I want us to be a family and for her as well as our unborn child to grow up not only together, but in a two parent household. I know you won't just accept my apology and move on like nothing happened but I will do whatever I have to for you to forgive me," I told him honestly. Besides work, I was miserable without Jarell and it was evident. Even my mother noticed it. She told me I needed to figure out what I was doing with myself because she was tired of seeing me walking around miserable.

"I'm willing to work on us, but I want you to realize my daughter isn't going anywhere. She has a huge picture of me and her mother in her room and I'm sure as she gets older, she's going to ask about her. So I need you to be prepared for the talks about Alicia. I'm sure they will occur and I will not deny my daughter any information about her deceased mother."

"I understand," I told him truthfully . I didn't know what it was like to lose a parent, let alone at the age of three and I didn't want to experience it. For the first time, I looked at Jarell and smiled. I hoped we could go only up from here because I was tired of not having him in my life.

Chapter Thirty One

Jonnae

Things had been calm lately, which was a surprise. I couldn't lie and say I wasn't happy about it though. It had been a long time since we had no drama in our family. I just laid the twins down for a nap and was separating clothes for laundry, when the doorbell rang. I wasn't expecting anybody and usually Rell, Boog or Michelle would call before they came by. I dropped the clothes on the floor before heading over to the door. Looking out the peephole, I thought I was seeing things. I opened the door and stared at the beautiful lady in front of me.

"Mom?" I questioned as tears welled in my eyes. If it weren't for her hazel like eyes, I wouldn't have recognized her. She cut her hair into a short Halle Berry hairstyle and it really fit her round face well.

"Hey Nae-Nae," she said, calling me by the nickname she gave me as a little girl. She hadn't called me that name in so long.

"Wow! You look amazing! Come in," I told her as I stood to the side. My mother looked good. I mean, she always looked good when she was clean but something about this time and the look she had in her eyes, made me feel like this was the last time she would be in rehab. "When did you get out?"

"I've been out for about three weeks. I wanted to get myself together before I came and saw you . I completed the program almost a month ago and found a job. I was just approved for a one-bedroom apartment and I moved in three days ago."

"Wow! I don't even know what to say. I'm really proud of you though. Seriously."

"Thank you. I know I've disappointed you several times in the past but this is it. I'm tired of being a failure to my children and my grandchildren. I know I wasn't the best mother, especially when you needed me the most. I promise to be the best grandmother to the twins. I'm sad I missed their first birthday though," she said. Two weeks ago, we gave the twins a huge first birthday party. It took us two days to go through the gifts and put everything away.

"It's okay. You're here now and that's all that matters. I just put them down for a nap so they'll be out for about two hours or so."

"Where's Ja'kahri?" she asked. "I want to thank him for footing the bill for my rehab stay this whole time."

"He's not here but he'll probably be home shortly. I'm

sure he'll be glad to see you. Unless you want to call him instead?"

"No, it's fine. I would rather surprise him. Do you need help with anything?"

"I'm actually just doing laundry. I'll probably give the twins something simple to snack on and cook dinner by the time they get up."

"How do you do that?" she asked.

"Do what?"

"Able to cook with the twins being awake? I used to have to do everything while you and your brother were sleeping," she said as she laughed.

I chuckled as I went back to separating clothes.

"It's easy since they both just sit there and let me do what I have to. I'll turn on a cartoon and they don't even pay me any mind. They only cry if they need a diaper change or hungry. Other than that, they are fine."

"You were definitely blessed because most people don't get one calm child, let alone two."

We shared another laugh and I had to admit, it felt good. I hadn't had a calm and relaxing time with my mother in so long, I almost forgot what it felt like.

"So tell me," she said. "what have you been up to since the last time I saw you?"

I thought about all we had been through the last two and a half months. I wouldn't dare tell her all of that because I wasn't trying to relive any of it.

"A whole bunch of shit," I said laughing. "I mean we've been through some life things but other than that, we have just been managing. I know I said it before, but I have really been thinking about going back to school in January.

I just have to convince Capo to let me put the babies in daycare. I haven't spoken to him about it. I guess I should and soon."

"I'll have to really prove myself because of my past but I'm willing to help in any way that I can," my mother told me.

"Thanks Ma."

Just as we finished our conversation, I heard Capo opening the front door.

"Babe," I called out. "Come in the kitchen." He didn't say anything as he walked in the kitchen before stopping in his tracks. My mother looked at him, and smiled as she walked towards him.

"Wow, Rita! You look great," he said hugging her tightly.

"I feel great. I was just telling Jonnae I wanted to thank you for paying for my rehab this time. I really appreciate it."

"Not a problem, Rita. I'm just glad to see you clean and I hope this was the last time going," he said. I looked at him then looked at my mom. I hoped she didn't take what he said offensive.

"Trust me, this is it. I've done enough damage to my kids and missed enough of my grandchildren's lives. I moved into my own apartment a few days ago and I've been working for the last couple of few weeks. I really am trying to get my life together and remain on the right track," she said. Something inside of me, made me believe her and I hoped that this wouldn't come back to bite me in the ass.

Capo hugged my mother again, before turning his

attention to me.

"Are you cooking tonight?"

"Yeah, I figured I would make garlic mashed potatoes, meat loaf and corn. Why?"

"Just asking. I got to run out and meet up with Boog but I wasn't going to grab something to eat if you were cooking."

"Well tell Boog to meet you here so he can see my mom. Maybe Michelle will stay here while y'all handle business," I said. I wanted them to come over because I wanted my mother to surprise Boog and I wanted her to see Michelle's belly. They found out they were having a little boy and Boog couldn't be happier. All he talked about was how much he wanted a son. We all knew this world didn't need another Jonathan Carter, especially one that acted just like him.

I filled up a basket of the twin's clothes and carried it down to the basement to throw in the washing machine. As soon as I finished, I grabbed my phone to call my brother. Capo and my mother were talking, so I walked away from them before placing the call. I didn't want Boog to hear my mother's voice.

"Wassup sis," he answered.

"What are you doing?"

"Shit, just waiting for your man to hit me up."

"Oh, he just got home. Why don't you and Chelle come over, that way Chelle can hang with me while you and Capo go out?" I said. I hoped he fell for it because I couldn't think of a good enough reason for them to come over.

"A'ight, let me ask her but I'm sure she'll agree to it ."

"Okay." We ended the call and I went back to the kitchen. "Boog said he's going to see is Chelle wants to stop by."

"Did you tell him I was here?" my mother asked.

"No."

"Good."

"Well I'll be downstairs until he comes," Capo announced as he gave me a kiss and took off. Looking at my mother sitting at my kitchen island, I was happy and felt complete; something I hadn't felt in years.

Chapter Thirty Two

Boog

It took a little convincing for me to get Michelle to go to Nae and Capo's house. She whined about how she didn't want me to leave but I told her at least Nae and the kids could keep her company while I handled business with Capo. She slid her semi swollen feet into her memory foam slippers that I had gotten her and pulled a hoodie over her head. Twenty minutes after Nae called me, we were heading out the door.

Fifteen minutes later, I pulled up to their house. I killed the engine and hand in hand, Michelle and I walked up to the front door. I rang the bell and waited for one of them to open it. I wasn't prepared for the person on the other side of the door.

"Mom?" I asked. She smiled and for a second, I felt like

the six-year-old boy who always melted at his mother's smile. I released Michelle's hand and embraced my mother tightly. I couldn't believe she was really standing in front of me and looking better than she ever had.

"Hi, son," she said. "Come on in." She stood to the side as Michelle and I walked in. The moment Chelle turned to the side, my mother wasted no time noticing her bulging stomach. "Am I expecting a third grandchild?" she asked with a wide smile. Both Michelle and I couldn't hold back our smiles.

"Yes, a little boy, who will be here in February," I told her.

"Aw, congratulations." She hugged me again then hugged Michelle. "Another grandbaby I can spoil to death. I guess Ja'kiyra will be the only granddaughter I'll have."

"Trust me mom, she's enough," Nae chimed in. We all laughed. Just as we calmed down, I heard the twins crying. "She must have known we were talking about her," Nae said as she took off up the stairs towards their room. I sat on the bar stool next to my mother as Michelle stood between my legs. I placed my hand under her hoodie and rubbed her stomach.

"When did you get out?" I asked my mom. She went on to tell me about her recovery, when she got out and what she was doing now. I was proud of my mom. I knew deep down inside was the woman she used to be when Nae and I were little. I sat and chopped it up with my mom as she played with Ja'kiyra and Michelle helped Nae cook.

"Aye, you ready?" Capo asked me as he came downstairs with Kahri.

"Yeah." I leaned in to kiss my mom and niece on the

cheek. I walked around the island to reach Michelle and kissed her cheek as well. "I'll be back," I told her. I kissed her again, kissed Nae and headed out with Capo.

"I'll be back, Ma," he shouted to Nae as he strapped Kahri in his high chair. She didn't say anything as we left.

"So what's the deal?" I asked as soon as we got in the car.

"Last I heard, Chauncey pled guilty to second-degree and was sentenced to twenty-years."

"Did he say why he took so long to turn himself in?"

"He said he wanted to spend time with his kids but Dee shot that down. She told me that he only spends like an hour a day with them, if that. It is what it is though, we're clear from that shit."

"That's what I like to hear," I told him. It was like take a breath of fresh air. Now I needed to handle the situation with Kitty. I was waiting for LaToya to call me to let me what going on . It was hard because I was tempted to go to her house and go off on her.

"What's up with that other shit though?" he asked me.

"What shit?"

"With that chick. LaToya mentioned the case but said she was having a hard time finding her. She said if she doesn't find her or doesn't get word from the lawyer representing the chick, she can have the case thrown out."

I didn't know if I should mention that I knew where she could be found or if I should just leave it alone.

"What's on your mind?" Capo asked me. I told him what I was thinking to get his opinion on what I should do. "If it were up to me, I would leave it alone. Why build a case against yourself? If she was serious about this shit, she would be fighting to build that case."

He made a valid point.

"Let's forget all that shit though," he said. "Let's make this money."

I dapped him up and we pulled off. I pulled bud and a dutch out of my pocket then began rolling up a blunt. I'm sure with everything that had been going on between us; this blunt was more than needed.

"I've been thinking," Capo said.

"About?"

"Going ahead and marrying your sister."

"Aren't y'all engaged?"

"Yeah, but I think it's time to put some wedding plans into motion."

"Has she started planning?" I asked while licking the dutch.

"I don't know."

"Start there. At least ask if she started planning it and go from there."

"Good looks."

I finished rolling the blunt and sparked it up. Just as I passed it to Capo, my phone vibrated. I pulled it out and noticed it was Knuck calling.

"Yo," I answered.

"Swing through if you can. I got this new movie I want you to check out," he said. I chuckled at his way of telling me he needed more work. That was a first but I understood.

"A'ight, give me like an hour or two and I'll be there."

"Yup."

We ended the call and I slid my phone back in my pocket.

"We got to make a pit stop," I told Capo as he passed me back the blunt. I explained to him what Knuck called for and he was down for it.

"You ever think about getting out of this shit?" he asked as we pulled up to the spot.

"All the time but I don't just want to quit without having a solid backup plan. I need to make sure I have another source of income. I have a child on the way and sitting around making Michelle bust her ass for our child isn't cutting it. As a man, I have to take charge and handle business," I explained.

"I definitely feel you. I have two little ones to look after and the last thing I need is your sister thinking that I'm not trying to do right by them or her."

I couldn't help but laugh because I knew how my sister was. I pulled out my phone and dialed Knuck's number to see where he was. I only traveled once with work since I been out but I preferred not to.

"Yo," he answered.

"Where you at?"

"Pulling up."

"A'ight." I ended the call and told Capo, I would be back. I climbed out and led Knuck up the second floor apartment where this shit was kept. I kept it wrapped up because the only person I sold to was Knuck and he always bought his shit whole. He followed behind me with his duffle bag. He dropped it on the floor as soon as we stepped in.

"Gimme five minutes," I told him. I grabbed the bag and headed to the back bedroom. I locked the door behind me and opened the bag. I trusted Knuck, so I didn't feel the need to have to count every single dollar. I eyed it before opening the safe and starting to quickly stack the money in there. Afterwards, I lifted the corner of the rug in the closet and started taking the bricks out of the floor. I stacked the ten in the bag for Knuck and put everything back, the way it was.

I zipped the bag closed and headed back out to the living room, where Knuck was sitting down on the sectional.

"Done," I dropped the bag in front of him and together; we walked out of the apartment. Once I got back to Capo's car, Knuck dapped me up, thanked me and went on about his business.

"Damn, that was quick," Capo said as I closed the door after I climbed in.

I chuckled. "I get in, handle shit and get out. No need to prolong shit."

"That's what I'm talking about."

As we pulled off I thought about my unborn son and what Capo said about getting away from this. I definitely wanted and needed to . My family depended on it.

Chapter Thirty Three

Michelle

I hadn't seen Boog smile as hard as he did when he seen his mother, since he found out we were having a little boy. I was close to my mom and couldn't imagine not being able to see her for months or years. I could barely go a day without talking to her. My father was another story. I was over trying to fix the relationship with him. It was what it was. Boog didn't speak about his mother often, but I know it bothered him not having her around.

His mother seemed happy to be around both of her children as well as her grandchildren. She kept looking towards my stomach and I couldn't wait for my son to be here so she could shower him with her love as well. I was glad to give her another grandchild.

"How have you been feeling, Michelle?" she asked me

as I was helping Nae peel potatoes.

"Okay. The tiredness is just starting to kick in but I relax a lot."

"How have you and Jonathan been?" I thought about the bitch that came by the house a few months ago and almost got upset again. I then remembered that we were working on moving forward and letting the past go. Things between us had been great and I wanted to keep it that way.

"We're doing good. Just taking everything a day at a time."

She was probably expecting me to go into detail, but I wasn't planning on it. I wanted to leave it where it was.

"That's good."

The kitchen became quiet and I shot a look over to Nae, who glanced at me and smirked. I hoped her mother didn't take offense to my lack of conversation but truthfully, I didn't know what to say to her. She always knew me as Jonnae's friend and I wasn't sure how she felt about me as her son's child's mother. I hoped she didn't feel any type of way.

"I'm going to go change baby girl, Nae," her mother announced. A part of me was glad to get a break from her. The quietness was almost unbearable.

"Okay."

She grabbed Kiyra and spoke to her in baby talk, all the way up the stairs.

"Nae, I think your mom may feel some kind of way towards me," I told her.

"Why do you feel like that?"

"I don't know. Something about the way that conversation went. It was like she wanted me to go into detail about Boog and I's relationship. Since I didn't, she might feel some kind of way."

She chuckled, "Girl you're over thinking. She's like that. She did the same shit about me and Capo. She just wants to be involved in everything so she asks questions to be nosey. Don't worry about it, trust, she'll be fine."

I took what she said and shrugged his mother off. I continued helping Nae cook until Kahri started to whine.

"Chelle, I'm gonna go exchange Kahri with Kiyra, so my mom can change him. Do you think you can finish peeling these potatoes for me? I'll come back and chop them up."

"Yeah that's fine." She smiled at me, washed her hands and took off. I watched as Nae moved around. This would be me in a few months, except I would only have one child. I had to give it to Nae because she never once complained about being tired. She hardly complained about doing a lot of things a mother does, and alone. I admired her for that and I only hoped I could be half the mother she was.

Within minutes, Nae was coming back down with Kiyra. She was flailing her little arms and laughing. I smiled at the sight and became even more excited for the birth of my son.

"Thank you," Nae said as she put Kiyra in her high chair and turned some cartoons on. She came back over to the kitchen and washed her hands again.

"How do you do it Nae?" I asked her.

"Do what?"

"Juggle motherhood, being a housewife and still keeping Capo happy."

She shrugged, as she put on the pot of water for the

potatoes and started chopping them up.

"I just do, like I told you, there is no book on parenting so you just learn to do it and go with it. When Capo is around, he helps me but most of the time, he's out handling his business and I'm here with the babies. I must say, I am grateful to be blessed with two easy going babies. They aren't the type that set each other off and they don't cry for no reason, so that helps a lot. When I first had them, I wasn't sure I would be able to do it, but I've been doing it well if I must say so myself. Now, I just want to go back to school to have something for myself and for my kids to be proud of me for," she said.

"I understand." I sat on the stool and watched her move around the kitchen. Her mother came back downstairs and sat Kahri on the counter.

"Ma, put him in his chair so he can watch TV with his sister," Nae told her. I looked at her mother, who looked like she wanted to protest but instead, did what Nae said before sitting next to me.

"So Michelle, do you plan on having a baby shower?"

I shrugged. "I want to but I haven't began planning one. I'm okay if I don't have one though. Between Jonathan, myself and my parent's, our son will be okay if we don't have a shower."

"Nonsense! You need to have one," she said.

"Mom! If she doesn't want a shower, she doesn't have to have one. Don't start trying to take over people's lives again. We had that discussion before."

She threw her hands up in surrender and stood up.

"Alright, alright. I'm heading out." She didn't say anything else as she grabbed her purse and walked out the door. Shortly after she left, Boog and Capo came back in.

"I just saw your mom speeding off, what happened?" Capo asked as he kissed the kids and Jonnae.

"Same shit she always does, trying to take over somebody else's parenting and tell them what they need to do. I shut that shit down. She had her chance to be a parent, now it's time for us to learn."

"You okay?" Boog asked me. I nodded and continued watching Nae. At first I was happy for their mom to shower my son with love. Now I was starting to wonder, if she was going to try and take over then tell me how to be a parent to my child.

Epilogue

Four Months Later…

I looked in the little mirror in the bathroom and stared at myself. I couldn't believe, I was about to get married. After talking to Nae, we agreed that we would just get married at the Justice of the Peace. Her mom had something to say but as always, Nae shut her down. I loved her mother but I hated when she tried to force her opinion on people. I didn't say much of anything because she wasn't my mother.

In a few minutes, I would be a married man and I was ready. Nae and I had been together long enough plus she had done so much to deserve to share my last name. We planned on having a blowout reception afterwards. A knock on the door, broke me from my thoughts.

"Yeah," I called out. Boog popped his head in the door and asked if I was ready. "Yeah, give me a second. I'll be right out." Both Michelle and Boog were going to be our witnesses. I took another deep breath before turning and leaving. I walked into the room, where the officiant stood waiting for me. I guessed Jonnae was still getting ready. As we waited, Boog straightened out my tie.

"You ready for this? This is the second biggest day of your life after the birth of the twins."

"Yeah man. It's been a long time coming. I love that girl more than life itself and I'm beyond ready to spend the rest of my life with her." I meant every word that I spoke to my boy.

"A'ight." Just as we finished the conversation, Jonnae walked down the small walkway with both Ja'kiyra and Ja'kahri Jr. on each side. I smiled at her. Her simple white Vera Wang mini dress, hugged her body nicely. Even with the small weight gain after having the twins, I still loved her body. She held her small bouquet tightly and as she made her way to me, she handed it to Michelle. Instead of repeating vows, we decided to give our own short versions. First, we were instructed to sign the marriage license before our actual mini ceremony.

"Jonnae, you may start with your vows," the officiant said. She looked me and I could see the tears in her eyes.

"Ja'kahri," she said with a shaky voice. "I love you and I knew you would be mine ever since the day I met you at the corner store." I couldn't help but chuckle at her. "I'm so glad to have you in my life. I couldn't have asked for a better man in my life as my other half and the father of my children. I'm glad that God put you in my life when he did because it is because of you that I was able to come as far as I have. I can't thank you enough for blessing me and choosing me to spend the rest of your life with."

If I could have kissed her right at this moment, I would have.

"Ja'kahri, you can now recite yours," he told me.

"Jonnae," I said as it took a deep breath. "When I laid eyes on you at the store, I just thought you would be the one who would make me chase you around forever but I knew I would do whatever to make you mine. Fortunately, you didn't make me chase you. Our friendship naturally flowed and turned into love. We've been through a lot but I wouldn't want to go through these trials with anybody else, except for you. You've blessed me with two beautiful children and another person I can call my brother. I love you unconditionally and I can't wait to spend my life with you." I wiped the two lone tears that slid down her face with my thumb.

"You may now-." Before he could finish, I had her face cupped in my hands and smashed my lips into hers. "Well, no need for me to finish."

Boog and Michelle clapped and the twins followed suit. Just like that, we were Mr. and Mrs. Ja'kahri Turner. I scooped up my children as we posed for Michelle and Boog to take pictures. I could easily be deemed as the happiest man alive.

***

Jonnae

I couldn't believe just that fast, I was now a married woman. My relationship with Capo wasn't perfect but I must say, over the last two and a half years, we have made it work. For the first time in the last year, we've had peace.

No extra females, no law enforcement, no drama; nothing and I was happy about that.

We walked out of the courthouse together and were heading to the house for a cookout. We thought about renting out a hall but decided on something more private with our friends and family. Twenty minutes later, we were pulling up to the house. I wanted to change into something more comfortable and warmer. For January, it was rather cool but I knew by the nightfall, it would be colder. Capo was going to grill everything early, so we could sit in the back breezeway to enjoy the food with everyone yet still remain warm.

"Babe, do you need anything from the store?" I asked him as I began heading upstairs to lay both of the sleeping children down. I was going to change into some sweats at least for now to run to the store.

"Just grab chips and drinks. Everything else is here."

"Okay." I threw on sweats, a plain tee, a hoodie and my sneakers, then grabbed my wallet and rushed out to the store. As I drove, I couldn't help but to steal glances at my ring. It was beautiful. I made it to Stop & Shop in no time. Luckily, it was still early so the market wasn't packed. I went straight to the snacks aisle. As I was putting the second case of soda into my carriage, I heard my name being called.

"Jonnae?"

I turned and came face to face with Shakeisha. I almost wanted to resort back to the seventeen year old teenager, who was hurt by her friend's actions and beat the shit out of her. She was lucky because the wife and mother in me, allowed me to keep my cool.

"Shakeisha."

"Wow! How are you?"

"Fine. I would love to sit here and chat with you, but I would be fronting like I like you, when truthfully, I would rather fuck you up right now. So to save you a trip to the hospital and me a trip to the police station, I'm just gonna leave." I grabbed the third case of soda and walked away. I didn't have time to fake the funk like everything was forgotten, when it wasn't.

"Actually," she said walking up behind me in the line, I was in cashing out. "I was trying to extend my condolences about Chink." I rolled my eyes.

"There is no need to extend condolences because he isn't my man."

"But wasn't he your ex?"

"Your point is?" I asked, turning around giving her my full attention. "Listen, I couldn't give a fuck about you or him. Go send your condolences to somebody who needs them, like his mother. Stop fucking talking to me." The cashier was looking at me and I was sure she was shocked that this was going on so early in the day, but she was pushing me . I wanted her to hurry and cash me out, so I could leave. Thankfully, Shakeisha didn't say another word and I was able to cash out and leave. I wasn't even going to bring this up to Capo. I wanted to keep our smooth sailing, just like it was. I was ready to get home and celebrate my marriage with my family. I was over the bullshit and planned on leaving it all behind.

Capo agreed to me putting the children into daycare so I would officially begin classes in September and I couldn't wait. This was something that I wanted for so long and was glad that my husband was supporting me going back. I couldn't be happier and this only confirmed I was ready to spend the rest of my life with this man.

***

Jarell

These last couple of months, raising Jaynell has been fun but I would be lying if I said it was easy. I was surprised at how much Jass had stepped up. Since that night we talked, she had changed completely and I loved it. She was hands on with Jaynell and my baby girl adapted to her well. Jass was a natural with the parenting thing and it made me that much happier that we would be welcoming our own daughter together, Ja'elle Amor Turner in two months.

Jaynell sometimes asked about Alicia and as promised, I made sure to remind her about her mother. I kept in touch with Alicia's mother and father. I also brought Jaynell by to see Alicia's mother twice a week. The bond they built was amazing. Jaynell seemed to bring Linda so much joy and I was glad for that. I had just finished getting Jaynell dressed so we could head over to Capo and Nae's to celebrate their wedding. I couldn't believe my brother was a married man but I was beyond glad that he had a wife like Nae. They deserved each other and seemed to balance each other out. I could only hope to have a love and build a family as strong as theirs with my children and Jasmine. After all I had been through in life, I felt like that was the least I deserved.

Alicia's ex boyfriend, Monroe was charged with accessory to commit murder. Once they replayed all of the phone calls that he placed, they noticed that he was the one who had put it in their heads that she stole the money herself. They never found the guy who actually pulled the trigger but with Monroe already being incarcerated, a lengthy sentence was tacked on. They had checked into the people who Monroe made the calls too, but they all were burner phones. It would have been better if the actual killer was in jail, but I was satisfied with Monroe remaining in jail for doing her dirty like that.

I prayed now that Alicia was completely at peace and I could only hope that I was making her proud with my raising of our daughter.

***

Boog

Witnessing my little sister getting married brought me over a sense of happiness. My sister had been through a lot in her young life and I was glad she was finally getting the happiness she deserved. I sat in the chair behind Capo as he grilled the meat.

"Jonathan!" I heard Michelle scream. I jumped out of my seat and dashed inside to find her standing in the kitchen, looking as if she had pissed on herself. She looked nervous as ever.

"What happened?"

"I-I think my water broke," she said with a shaky voice.

"Oh shit. Um, uh, shit!"

"Do something!" she said as she gripped her stomach. A look of pain spread across her face.

"Okay, come on," I stood behind her and guided her towards the door.

"I want to take a shower first," she said wincing again.

"As much pain as you're in, are you sure that's what you want to do?"

"Whatever! Get me to the damn hospital," she yelled. I called out to Capo in hopes that he knew what I was supposed to do.

"What happened?" he asked, coming inside.

"Her water broke and I have no idea what the fuck I'm supposed to be doing." He chuckled and as much as I wanted to laugh with him, this wasn't a laughing matter.

"Where's her bag?"

"At the house."

"No, it's in the trunk," she said rubbing her stomach. "I knew he would be making his appearance soon and I didn't want to be unprepared."

"At least somebody is ready," Capo said. Just as we made it out front, Jonnae pulled up.

"Her water broke," I told her before she could even ask any questions.

"Oh shit! Okay, go to the hospital. If you need me, let me know. I'll be here," she said. I knew she wanted to go but leaving Capo alone with the kids wasn't going to happen.

I finally got Michelle in the car and tried to help her breathe through the pain. I wished I could take her pain away because the look on her face had me ready to cry for her. In eight minutes flat, we pulled up to the emergency room entrance. The moment we walked in and they noticed her wet leggings, they immediately took her back and hooked her up to different monitors. Luckily, it was during the day, so her OBGYN was already working. The moment she was undressed and in the hospital bed, the doctor was knocking on the door.

"Good Afternoon, Michelle. How are you feeling?" Dr. Reid asked her as she washed her hands.

"In pain! Everything hurts," she said. Looking at her, for once, I felt helpless.

"Alright, let me check you out and I will let you know if you dilated enough along to get pain medications." She put gloves on and had Michelle prop her legs up. I looked between what she was doing and Michelle's face. "Looks like you're just about five centimeters and baby boy is completely head down. You can get the epidural if you would like."

"Yes!"

I chuckled.

"Okay, I'll put that in for you and get you as comfortable as possible." When the doctor left, Michelle turned on her side and stared at me. I walked over and tried to comfort her as much as I could until the doctor came back with her meds.

After six hours of kicking, screaming, and hand squeezing, my little man Jonathan Carter Jr. made his entrance into the word at 9:42pm on January 23rd weighing five pounds seven ounces, eighteen inches long. The feeling I felt as that moment was indescribable. I was overjoyed and couldn't thank Michelle enough for blessing me with my youngin. I kissed her so many times, I'm almost positive she was tired of them. He looked just like I did when I was a baby, except he had a little more hair than I did and his was curly. I couldn't stop staring at him. When I rubbed my finger across his cheek, he opened his eyes and I swore I saw a smile creep across his little face. I never felt more blessed than I did at that moment.

I hadn't heard from Kitty in a few months. The last time I heard from her, she had called me crying about how she had a miscarriage. Being honest, and as sad as it was, a part of me was happy because I didn't even want the possibility of her child being mine. Plus, karma was a bitch. She thought she was going to have me locked up for so bogus shit.

I looked down at my son again.

"Thank you, Ma! I truly can't thank you enough."

She smiled at me. I smiled back at her, kissed her forehead and told her to get some rest. She wasn't lying. It wasn't easy loving us Carter's but we were well worth the fight. One thing about us though, when we love, we love hard and that was one thing you didn't have to worry about with us. Our love never had to be questioned.

"Ya know," she spoke up with her eyes closed. "I wondered if it was worth it but that little man right there proved that it is worth, Loving A Carter."

The End...

About The Author

Leondra LeRae grew up in Providence, RI. She is the mother of a little girl who is her pride and joy. She has dreams of becoming an OBGYN but enjoys writing in her free time. At 19, she self-published her first urban fiction novel

At 20 years old, Leondra signed to SBR Publications where she released National Best Seller; Official Street Queen.

Feel free to interact with her
Like her fan page:
www.facebook.com/AuthorLeondraLeRae
Follow her on Twitter: www.twitter.com/LeondraLeRae
Instagram: www.instragram.com/leo_xo
Email: authorleondralerae@gmail.com

Select Any Other of Her Reads on Amazon at:
www.amazon.com/author/leondralerae

CPSIA information can be obtained
at www.ICGtesting.com
Printed in the USA
LVHW020213150620
658044LV00010B/1036